CW00927505

To Jacky,

LIBERTY ANGEL

JENNIFER LYNCH

Best Wishes,

Jennifer Lynch

ISBN 978-1-7394956-3-3

All characters and events in Liberty Angel are
entirely fictional and
any resemblance to any person living or dead is
purely coincidental.

Foreword

Liberty Angel was written to help women to find

divine strength and courage.

Liberty Angel

CONFESSION

Gemma sat next to the scorching fire. If her skin burned, she didn't care because she was cold. When her jeans started to smoke with the intense heat, she decided to give in to her sensible side and move away from it. The flames which were far more interesting than the game show, hypnotized her. The fire which now resembled witches and wizards, lept out celebrating its own unique rhythm then quickly faded into embers. The flames held a special kind of magic, as if casting a spell or a wish which Gemma desperately needed as her life was about survival. Sitting in front of the fire had become a reminder of her mortality. A place to examine her feelings and explore her life purpose. Did she have direction, or was she merely existing? Was she a good parent, or had she been selfish to leave Tony? Would her children have had a better life if they had stayed together? Gemma continued to share her thoughts with the fire in the hope of a greater force coming into play when she focused her intentions. Could the fire's magic bring the transformation she so desperately sought?

It was nine pm, and Gemma quickly surveyed the room for what she needed to do before bedtime. The children's school bags lay on the floor. She wanted to look at their homework, but she was too tired. The girls had declared 'there wasn't any reading tonight,' so Gemma chose to believe them. She quickly moved the bags on to the table so they would remember them in the morning. The fire turned to a gentle heat which no longer alarmed the cat, who sprawled out on the rug in front of the hearth. Brave cat Gemma muttered as she realised her legs stung.

Gemma didn't want to hurt herself. She wanted love, but the abuse was a mild kind of pain which kept her alive. It was easier to burn her legs than to acknowledge the emptiness she'd felt since her divorce from Tony. The past two years had been trying. Learning to be independent and finding the confidence to bring up two children on her own had been harder than she expected.

Gemma first met Tony when she was in her twenties, and they were only married for two years. She relied on him to take care of their finances because that's what he wanted. She thought it was a shame that Tony wouldn't allow her to help, but he wanted to take full responsibility for the family budget. During their last year together, communication had become a problem. She often tried to engage him in conversation, but the harder she tried, the more he withdrew into a world of his own. She was unsure when, or how they lost each other, but they did. Their small niggles turned into more substantial disagreements, and Gemma quickly realised they'd grown apart. They were two separate people walking in different directions, and the gap between them had become too wide to bridge.

Gemma felt separating from Tony was her only choice. Even if she felt alone as a single parent, at least she'd be able to make her own decisions. It had become her responsibility to take care of the girls, and sometimes the process was tedious. Starting her life from scratch was hard with little family support and very few friends, except John who always listened to her when she visited him at the weekends.

Gemma decided to visit John on Saturday. He had two children who were the same age as the girls. She was in love with him, and she thought he felt the same way, but he couldn't express his feelings. This was easier than facing the truth, because John knew that he wasn't in love with Gemma, but he did consider her a good friend. Gemma was convinced John was her soul mate, and they were destined to be together. They had so much in common "they were meant to be," and it was merely a matter of time.

When Gemma suddenly appeared on John's doorstep, he was always pleased to see her, and she was always met with a hug and kiss. They would often talk for hours, putting the world to right while they sat at his kitchen table. They spent so many hours engaged in lengthy conversations that Gemma thought her world had opened to a whole new level. Over time, the conversations continued to grow along with their friendship. She was also greeted by aromatic cooking smells of a meal simmering on the hob, which was a bonus! Whenever she thought about John, she felt excited because he knew how to engage her, plus he was a great cook. She loved him cooking, because all she had to do was sit down and chat to him and something delicious would appear. He would often include her in his meal by adding extra ingredients because he wanted her to stay. 'Taste this,' he said one day as he spooned it into her mouth, and she let him because it was fun and something Gemma had never experienced. It made her laugh and brought them closer together. Intimacy was something that Gemma had never experienced, not with Tony. They'd had a sexual relationship, but this kind of intimacy was entirely different. It was fun because her life consisted of endless trips to school, listening to her children read, or teaching them long division. Gemma craved closeness not sex and if people didn't understand this, it was their problem. Had anyone the right to judge her? Her connection with John was special and it was on a whole new level.

Gemma hated the word divorced. It made her uncomfortable. The word stuck in her throat and brought her pain. It reminded her of loose women, a failed marriage, and being a social outcast. She thought about all the other women struggling on their own as they tried to find their place in a world which was cruel to divorcees. She was now a woman with raw emotions and part of her felt like she was dying. She could no longer see a daffodil nodding its head to tell her Spring had arrived. Gemma was lost. Her only warmth existed in her heartfelt conversations with John which lifted her and made her smile. He had become the light in her heart which continued to glow through the day until the fire turned to ashes. He was her hope of a new life where she could experience love again, and her life would eventually return to normal!

Gemma looked in the mirror, at 32, she was still young and attractive, but she recognised that she needed to smile more. Her hair was long wavy and dark and her eyes which she inherited from her mother were hazel. They were often referred to as green because they were hard to distinguish. The people she met seldom looked at her for long, sensing her sadness. Gemma noticed they found it hard to communicate because they continually made assumptions about her status. If something didn't register with them, it didn't exist, and since her divorce, it was worse! She was often referred to as Mrs, which was wrong because she'd changed Mrs to Ms months ago, but they always got it wrong in the Council offices, and she was tired of correcting them.

Sometimes Gemma would telephone her good friend Adrian, a spiritual man who had studied Buddhist meditation. He'd been Gemma's spiritual teacher and friend for several years. He always gave her great advice and made sense when others didn't. He had a way of listening, which put her entirely at ease. From what she understood, Adrian had spent lengthy periods in spiritual retreats in silence. Gemma thought this was incredible. When they chatted last night, Adrian explained to her that to be happy in relationships she needed to lower her expectations. Gemma didn't want to attract someone with the wrong intentions because she was looking for love and she didn't want to abandon her ideals. It was stupid to lower her expectations when the man of her dreams was out there. She was a dreamer, but she wanted to hold onto that. The thought of a better future with someone who really loved her, kept her going and besides John and her were becoming closer!

The following morning was cold and windy, and Gemma searched her clothes rail for something to wear. She chose a baggy jumper and jeans because later that day she would be collecting wood for the fire, so her attire had to be practical.

Gemma had a great figure being a size twelve and in good proportion. Her waist had thickened slightly since having her children but not to the extent anyone would notice! She was always on the move, which kept her weight off. There was a routine of housework, car trips, plus she was also looking for a job. It sometimes felt as if she was stuck in an ongoing battle without any let-up. She craved a day in bed because it was the same old routine, day in, day out, without a break unless Tony had the girls. Her ex-husband made things worse by his continual criticism of the way she managed the children. Although he didn't have control over her friendships, he would still put his opinions forward whenever he had the chance. If she listened to Tony's views, he would make her feel inadequate, so it was sensible to have as little communication with him as possible. She knew the children enjoyed seeing their father but there was no way that she'd ever go back there! Despite Tony's criticism, she felt the girls were making steady progress. They had both settled into their new schools and had adjusted well to living in their new home at the cottage.

The most important thing was that they appeared happy. If there were any problems about school, Gemma felt it right that she should talk to Tony, but she tried to avoid this because she knew that he'd be unpleasant.

Today, after Gemma had dropped the children off at school, she was relieved to have time to herself. She walked across the wooden floorboards, which creaked as if they had a life of their own. It was strange because Gemma had never noticed the creaking when the children were home. She sat down on a chair and began to look at the job page of the local newspaper that she'd picked up at a nearby shop. It wasn't a suitable time of year to look for work on the run-up to Christmas. The paper was very slim, so she decided to look at jobs again after the school holidays and continue with the many household jobs. How could two children go through so many clothes in a week? If she worked as well, it could prove to be difficult with so much housework. Still, there were only two more days until the weekend, and Tony was having the girls, so at least she could have a break. She didn't see her old friends often because they were also Tony's friends, and they were rarely in touch. Gemma missed the social side of being a couple because there were no longer invitations to barbeques meals or parties. Everything had been quiet on the social front, but there was a chance that John might be without his children this weekend, so they could spend some time together. She hadn't heard from him, so she didn't want to get her hopes up, but she was sure that he was free. John was always anxious when he had his children which was hardly surprising because they were a handful. They usually ran up and down the stairs rather than walking and they fought over everything! John tried to stop them by asking them to calm down, but they continued to do what they wanted as if they hadn't heard him. Their arguments were noisy, and they made Gemma feel uncomfortable because John spent most of his time trying to get his children under control and there was little time for them to chat.

John's daughter Milly had straight shoulder-length blonde hair and big brown eyes. She also had her father's enchanting smile. When the girl smiled, her face revealed two sweet dimples which gave her the appearance of a permanent smile! But John's son Steven was quite the opposite; he took things to heart. He didn't like his father's teasing because he was sensitive. Steven was tall for his age but skinny. Milly would continually tease her brother, and he'd get annoyed. The girl was young and bright, and she sometimes used her intelligence in the wrong way. She enjoyed having a dig at Steven because it made her feel superior. When the children disrupted the household, their chats in the kitchen had to take a backseat. Gemma was sad that Milly behaved like this. Had she learned how to tease from her father?

Saturday came, and Gemma was relieved that she finally had time for herself. Tony picked up the girls and packed their bags into the car.

'Right, I'll bring them back Sunday about six then,' Tony said abruptly. Gemma noticed that he was still very unpleasant, and she felt that he was resentful of her. She didn't want him back in her life, and she knew it was unlikely that he would want her, but it was a shame they couldn't be friends. In the future, they would be able to talk because it would be better for the children. It had been her choice to leave, and she knew Tony would always be a little angry about her decision, but he needed to forgive her and move on because life was too short to hold grudges!

. . . .

Gemma stood on John's doorstep with her stomach churning. He'd better be home she muttered as she tentatively rang the bell. John was a self-employed product designer who was talented and creative. Gemma was fascinated by his abilities, particularly his furniture designs. He was continually busy working from home or looking after his children, so it was hard for him to meet his clients, but he managed to juggle things well and he was already successful.

'Look at this, wow, that's incredible. You're going to be famous one day,' Gemma often told him, but he just laughed at her.

'I doubt it Gem, but who knows, you might be!' he often replied, with an enchanting smile.

Gemma rang the bell again. Why was he taking so long to answer she pondered as her heartbeat with anticipation. Should she quickly walk away? She hadn't been invited over. Was she imposing? She knew that she was, but when he answered the door, John always appeared pleased to see her.

John's Edwardian house had three bedrooms, each a decent size. Gemma thought it would be an incredible house if it was redecorated, but it hadn't been touched for years. Part of the property was modernised, which was great, but on rainy days the wallpaper in the living room smelt damp which Gemma found concerning!

Mozart bellowed from the front windows which had been left slightly open. John had a fantastic collection of music which was still growing. He enjoyed modern pop, classical and jazz music and Gemma was often greeted by something new and different! She took a couple of deep breaths and sighed. Why was he taking so long to come to the door? Was he busy or did he have a visitor. Had Lulu stayed over. She'd done that before! Gemma looked down and noticed her hands were shaking. Then she heard him approaching.

'Hi, come in,' John said casually, as he politely stood aside to allow her to enter. Gemma loved John's welcome. She wanted to sit with him and unwind to his music because nothing else mattered while she was there. His house had become her relaxation zone!

'Where are the kids?' she asked, hoping they were with their mother. Gemma knew she should be getting on with something herself, decorating shopping or finding new friends, instead of spending hours chatting to John, but he drew her like a magnet. The more she tried to pull away from him, the harder it became. She realised that she'd become attached to him and continually arriving on his doorstep wasn't the best idea. Still, she couldn't stop herself doing it. It was wrong to keep encroaching on his space because he had hardly any free time, but she still had to go, even if he pushed her away.

Mozart continued to echo through the Edwardian house bringing the old place to life, while the sun shone through the open windows creating a special kind of ambience. The music was so much louder inside, and Gemma quickly surveyed the sink, which was stacked to the top with dishes, which John had ignored because he was preparing lunch. A fantastic aroma of basil and tomatoes filled the kitchen which made Gemma hungry. He walked to his cooker and added Worcester sauce, 'no tomato dish should be without it,' he said.

Gemma began telling him her news. It sounded boring discussing her children's' week at school when nothing much had happened, but she couldn't think of anything better to say. She waited a while for a response from him, but instead of replying to her, John began talking about his week at work. He enthusiastically explained how his work colleague, a slender and attractive woman had been chatting him up.

"She has such an amazing body!' he told her.

'That's because she hasn't had children.' Gemma thought, feeling slightly sick. She felt jealousy brewing from an unfamiliar place and wondered why John was telling her this. Surely, he realised how insensitive he was. Her friends had often made compliments about her body, but she felt insecure about it. John was making her feel uncomfortable, and she once again considered making a hasty exit, when he quickly pulled her out of her thoughts and started talking about something else.

'Hey Gem, I'm having a party tonight. I've got to get the place cleaned up. I'm inviting about ten people. I don't know if everyone will make it but come if you can and please bring something to drink?' shouted John as he grabbed the vacuum cleaner from the cupboard and hastily began to clean.

Gemma didn't want to go to a party. She felt shocked that John was having one. Why couldn't they be on their own this evening? She knew that he had friends from work that she'd never met, and it made her uneasy. He'd also invited some friends who lived nearby, but Gemma didn't know any of them apart from Louise who had already proved to be a nightmare! Gemma lived five miles away and living out of town kept her a little distanced. She didn't want to share John with other people because they had a special relationship, and she felt the party would be challenging. Did her whole life have to revolve around this man? But if she walked away, she'd be isolated? There was her friend Adrian, but he had recently moved away, and they only spoke occasionally on the phone. Time flew when she was looking after the children, and she gave them all the love she could, but she still craved adult conversation, and John provided this. He was articulate and intelligent and had many qualities she admired, but his greatest asset was that he was great with his children. John loved them and had compromised his career by doing most of his work from home. It was challenging work, and sometimes Gemma could see that he had a short fuse but who could blame him? How could she be judgemental when she found it difficult being a parent herself. She wasn't working apart from the occasional little cleaning job, one morning a week. Gemma wondered if it was worth it, but at least it gave her some money to call her own. She pretended to herself that money wasn't everything because it was easier than admitting she missed the advantages. If she found a job it would make her and the girls' lives easier!

Gemma didn't want to go to the party, but she didn't want to miss an opportunity to be close to John! If she stayed home, he could easily slip into the arms of someone else and she'd be gutted. Part of her knew it was unlikely that they'd ever have a full relationship because she was quickly realising that she knew little about specific areas of his life. Gemma hadn't met many of John's friends or work colleagues. When he talked about his children or people at work she still listened attentively. He was always keen to share his ideas and designs in which she was genuinely interested. They were incredible.

John explained that a couple of months ago he'd been offered a job designing the furnishings for a new bar opening in North London. The Company had a chain of entertainment venues across the UK, so there was enough work to keep him busy for months on end. He would also advise the company on the layout, lighting and health and safety issues. Several weeks ago, he had asked Gemma if she'd like to go with him to London to their pre-launch party. The bar would open the following evening. Gemma thought long and hard about this because she had to make alternative arrangements for the girls but going to London was a new experience and something she didn't want to miss. When they met outside the Angel tube station, John had already been in London for several hours. He'd travelled up earlier to attend a meeting. When they arrived at the restaurant, the owners gave them a warm welcome and complimentary coffee, followed by nibbles with their architect and the other designers who were involved in the project.

Gemma was staggered by John's ability to achieve so much in such a short space of time. He must be proud to be part of this team she thought. She found the furnishings fascinating, especially the chairs, which worked well with their new fifties theme. She'd put herself out coming to London for John, but she was in awe of the project and thought he deserved support. People naturally assumed she was his girlfriend, and they smiled graciously at her while Gemma took every opportunity to stand close to John or take his arm, playing the part well. Let them think that she thought because she was as near as damn it! But, while Gemma was listening to him discussing their achievements, she once again realised how little she had to say. When John was more home-based, they sometimes discussed their children because they attended the same school and there was plenty to talk about, but whatever she said today would be out of place because he was mixing with a lot more women through his work. He now preferred to speak about his work and creative ideas most of the time and it became obvious to her that he'd become distant. Did his female colleague have some sort of crush on him? It made her feel wretched, but what could she do? She needed to break away from the friendship, but they had become so familiar it was impossible. Being her best and only friend, he was the person she shared everything with, and he knew it. It was an impossible situation and she felt emotionally tortured. If she didn't see him again, she would be lonely. Although she loved it at the cottage, she missed the girls when they were at school. She also wanted to spend time with adults. She tried to remember what it was like going out socially with her ex, had she enjoyed any of it? Was this life she had chosen any better than her previous life? She'd always considered her social life with Tony was sadly lacking but had she been wrong? Most of her memories about their socialising were of his firm's Christmas dinners or occasional outings. Neither of them had that many friends but the ones they had were the parents of their children's friends. With Tony being a solicitor, he had many business connections, so they were lucky enough to attend functions or meals at their houses. She wouldn't describe the couples that went along to these evenings as her friends! They were business acquaintances. While they were married, she'd visited many places and in truth, some of it was enjoyable. The problem now was her money was so tight, although she had her freedom, she still felt restricted.

One of her friends who was also their hairdresser had said to her, 'we don't want a life, we want a lifestyle.' The hairdresser was right, she did want a lifestyle! It had been a hard choice for her to leave but one that she had been forced to make. It was sometimes difficult for people to understand why she decided to go. She felt emotional pain which was hard to express to others. It didn't feel like happiness, but it certainly wasn't regret because there was a feeling of relief! Gemma often looked at herself in the mirror at home and said yep; I've done it. Now I'm free to do what I like, apart from the clocks which govern time, time for breakfast, time for lunch, time to collect the children, time to do their homework, time to put on the washing machine, paying attention to the electric metre, time to make sure they have gone to bed. Time for an hour's rest or chill out in front of the television, then time for bed! Every day was the same and this was her life!

THE PARTY

John walked from the kitchen to the living room, dragging the vacuum cleaner behind him and began cleaning while they were chatting. He threw the cushions off the chairs onto the floor to vacuum the sofa. He's thorough, thought Gemma who was surprised that a man would go to all that trouble. But she had learnt during their friendship that John never did anything by half! This was one of the qualities she admired because although his life wasn't easy, he tried so hard. Starting a new job and looking after two children had cause him to have money difficulties. In all, it was a miracle that he managed to juggle things. Gemma wondered how long he could sustain this energy. It had been her experience that female single parents supported other single parents, but what about male single parents, who was there for them? Gemma decided that she'd continue to be friends with him, wherever their friendship went and for however long it lasted. It was painful having feelings for him, especially when he constantly referred to his work colleague as a brilliant professional with a fantastic figure but there was little, she could do about that!

Gemma reluctantly decided to go to the party but planned not to drink so she could at least drive home and avoid complications. The cost of a taxi was expensive, so she had little choice. It was either wine or a taxi. She knew that she'd want to go home because it was great to be in her own bed when the children were with their father so she could have a lay in.

Gemma was soon standing on John's doorstep, wearing a nice pair of blue jeans and a red top, and ringing his bell. She hated the way she had made herself so dependent on him, but she loved what lay the other side of his front door. Then she remembered that Louise was also coming to the party, which would be difficult because she was continually making a play for John. Worse still, he loved it. They called her Lulu at the local pub because they knew her well! Lulu was an attractive and bubbly brunette who was slightly overweight but in a seriously cuddly way which Gemma thought took nothing away from her appeal! The girl was intelligent and lively, which impressed John because they were able to discuss the things he enjoyed. They talked for hours about their favourite poets, Keates, Blake and other modern poets that were unknown to Gemma. She found herself wanting to drop into their conversations, but she didn't want to make a fool of herself. She knew so little. Worse still Lulu lived around the corner.

In recent weeks, the young woman had become quite a threat to Gemma and her presence made Gemma uncomfortable. Lulu didn't have children, so she turned up at John's house whenever she felt like it! John would say that Louise had stayed the previous night, and she was often there until late morning. Gemma wondered if John was sleeping with her, but somehow, she doubted it because Lulu was already in a committed relationship with John's best friend! Not that it would have put him off. Gemma questioned John's scruples when it came to his sexual relationships with women because he'd made it obvious to her that he was a free spirit! John enjoyed Louise's teasing, and it was clear to Gemma that they shared the same sense of humour. They had frequent conversations from which she was excluded which left her feeling inferior because she hadn't been to university. Louise had an English Degree, and John had a degree in Product Design, however, he always said he'd gained his skills through trial and error. Even if he played it down, Gemma noticed they had many things in common, and they talked for hours about subjects she knew little about.

John quickly opened the door, then disappeared for a few minutes. His other local friends had already left their homes to meet at their usual pub, and he told Gemma they should go and join them and have a few drinks there before the party. Gemma wasn't keen on this idea because she wanted to get on with the party so she could drive home before it got too late, but she reluctantly agreed to go because it was around the corner. It was the pub that John popped in with Louise for the occasional drink. Gemma had a strong resistance to the bar because it was pokey and scruffy and in need of a refit! Gemma felt embarrassed by her effort to dress up because dressing down would have been more appropriate. She wondered what Tony would think of this place. She felt ashamed that it was so dowdy, and she swore that she'd never be dragged here again!

Gemma reluctantly sat down on a long-cushioned seat at the back of the pub because she wanted to dissolve in the corner. There were several locals at the bar who looked elderly and a couple of young men playing on a fruit machine who didn't bother to look up or acknowledge them. They seemed frustrated by the device because it wasn't paying out! There was no music playing, and the only sounds Gemma could hear were the sounds of the fruit machine as it whirled through its games.

Gemma sipped her lager and asked John when he thought Louise was arriving. She wanted the party to start rather than spending the evening in a run-down pub. They had waited for her for over an hour, and Gemma was bored. She'd done the wrong thing by coming, especially if it was a party where no-one was coming! Louise eventually appeared. She was in a terrible mood, and she walked straight over to talk to her, uttered a few words about needing to go home and change then disappeared! Gemma couldn't believe it! They had waited all this time, and she had left without an explanation!

'Where's Lulu gone?' she asked John.

John said he thought Lulu was unhappy with her clothes, so she went home to change! Louise finally resurfaced about half an hour later, wearing an identical red blouse to Gemma!

'What do you think of my top?' asked Louise with a smile.

Gemma tried not to react. What was the matter with her? Why did she behave like this? Lulu always wanted attention, and she enjoyed making people angry. Did she like seeing the reactions of others and laugh at their expense? But when you questioned her about her life, she was 'edgy.' Gemma had also discovered that she smoked a fair amount of weed. That was why her behaviour was so variable!

Gemma felt uncomfortable as she quickly came to realise this group lived in a different world to her. But what could she do? John was her best friend, so it would seem rude not to stick it out. It wasn't easy, especially as Louise had already wound her up by not only wearing a matching top but drooling over John. Their laughter was audible in every corner of the pub, and Gemma began to look for another seat further away which was a challenge in a bar the size of her living room!

Gemma looked at her watch, it was 10.30 pm, her usual bedtime. She felt tired after her week with the girls, but she didn't want to be a killjoy and leave before the party started. John told her that more of his friends were arriving soon. Gemma began to feel very apprehensive and continued to have thoughts about leaving. Why was Rob with Lulu when she was such a flirt? Was Rob just useful because he gave her somewhere to live while she was unemployed?

Rob, who had bright sparkly eyes, was tall, skinny, and knowledgeable. Gemma didn't know him very well, but she already thought he outshone Louise who understood the odd poem but had terrible manners. Rob worked full-time in Bicester, which was quite a drive from home. Every day he brought back money to pay the mortgage. Gemma quickly realised that Rob could have his choice of women and thought it strange that such an attractive man would wait for Louise. She was obviously unreliable and enjoyed the attention of other men. Despite this, Rob appeared to care about her. Rob explained he was tired of waiting for Lulu for hours and repeating, 'are you coming?' But he seldom got mad because he had developed a way of not caring! Gemma guessed that he was biding his time until their relationship fizzled. Why is he so weak, Gemma thought in total disbelief! Whatever went on in their heads, certainly wasn't the same as what went on in hers, when she had to constantly consider the girls.

At last, they walked back to the house to meet John's work friends. John put on some dance music and a small group strolled in. Gemma stared at them. He often talked about how marvellous they were, but she couldn't believe these were the people he referred to. After twenty minutes of trying to chat with them, she realised they were incredibly dull, and she had nothing to say.

John began talking to two of the men and a girl about music. It was his favourite subject after design, and they appeared interested as they worked their way through his shelf of CDs in awe. Gemma knew John so well she could almost predict his words. Fortunately, there didn't seem to be a woman with a fantastic figure within the group, and she relaxed slightly. Gemma knew that any woman who interacted with John was a potential threat but until now, she hadn't realised how many women that might be. Gemma felt threatened by John's friends and colleagues and wanted to retreat to the safety of her cottage, but she reminded herself she had to stay focused because Louise was turning on the charm.

Gemma started to feel insecure and wished the ground would swallow her up. She thought about sneaking out of the door and hoped no-one would notice. But she then decided to stay because that's what good friends do, stick around. But it wasn't easy when she felt lousy, so she went in search of some red wine! If she drank more than a glass, she'd be unable to drive home, which caused another dilemma, but she needed to numb her feelings.

The wine was excellent, and Gemma soon began to relax. She poured herself another glass and realised she wouldn't be able to drive home. As the evening progressed, Gemma gave herself her own bottle and was rapidly drinking it. She had placed it on top of the mantelpiece in the dining room away from the others, so no-one knew she had it. They weren't interested in coming in this room as they were all in deep conversation in the lounge area. The chat was about politics and economics. Gemma perked up because she knew a little about politics and eagerly walked into the lounge to stand on the edge of the group. She waited for a break in the conversation so she could join in but then realised it wasn't going to happen! She was amazed that despite drinking so much, John and his friends still managed to have an in-depth conversation. They were unaware of her presence. Was she invisible?

'Yes, voting for the smaller parties is a waste of time. They are a laughingstock that party, why do they bother,'

Gemma heard one of the men in the group remark. 'As if anyone cares that much about the environment!'

She felt disgusted by their comments. The group were so unaware of her that her desire to join them quickly left her. Gemma looked at all the empty glass bottles and wondered if they would ever reach a recycling bin? She'd talk to John about it when he was sober, surely, he wasn't as unaware as them, or was he?

Why do I have to be always so damn sensible, she sighed, feeling annoyed. She was trying to have fun but found it impossible to be herself in the company of these people.

John noticed Gemma was standing on her own and came over to her.

'Are you alright, Gem?' he asked.

'Yes, I'm ok,' she replied.

'They're all going home soon,' he continued reassuringly.

Half an hour later it was just John, Louise, Rob, and empty bottles of wine. John suddenly put on his light denim jacket and declared that he was going to the off licence to buy yet more drink!

'More wine? Do we need it?' asked Gemma, who felt that it was a terrible idea to keep on drinking! If she had any more, she'd find it difficult to go home, even in a taxi! John soon returned with another four bottles and began to fill up everybody's glasses. Gemma felt slightly sick as she noticed Lulu enjoying John's attention. Her red blouse which had been unbuttoned further, now revealed her fabulous cleavage. John was fully absorbed as his eyes roamed her breasts.

Children thought Gemma! Lulu knows nothing about kids, so if I drop that into the conversation, then John will chat to me and stop talking to Louise! Gemma drew several deep breaths, but again, nothing came out! She felt disappointed but realised that she was fighting a losing battle. She wasn't going to gain John's attention certainly not tonight. Louise was like a tarantula spider reaching out in every direction. She was building a web to catch him, and he appeared to be happy staying right where he was. Lu looked so charming with her black eyelashes and long blonde hair, which attractively bounced around her shoulders. At times like this, Gemma realised she both loved and hated being a single parent because part of her wanted to engage in conversation with adults again and be charming and stimulating but she couldn't think of what to say. Powerful women were an enigma to her, but she craved that power. She thought being a mother wasn't at all-interesting or exciting, and it left her frustrated. It appeared rude to butt in on their conversation, especially as she had started to feel giddy and might just start babbling rubbish! She went to sit on the sofa because she felt exhausted and wanted to close her eyes. Where was Rob? He'd been missing for some time. Did he care what was going on with John and Louise. She felt it was fair enough if they were good friends, but Lu's flirting made her feel awkward and abandoned. This party was proving to be her worse nightmare!

Gemma looked in her purse and saw she didn't have enough money for a taxi. She quietly edged her way towards the front door deciding she'd walk home despite it being a long way. Anything was better than staying where she was!

'Where are you going?' John asked, sounding a little shocked that she should leave without saying goodbye!

'Well, I thought I might make a move now,' said Gemma.

'No, don't do that, stay,' he replied with appealing eyes.

'Rob is here now. Look he's at the door.'

Gemma felt deeply sorry for Rob. He was always so quiet with the mannerism of an obedient dog. He had obviously become resolute to it all. He sat down next to Gemma on the sofa and explained that he'd been in the garden having a cigarette.

'I thought you'd gone home,' said Gemma, with a smile.

Rob smiled back, then gave her a long look and then spoke softly.

'I was thinking about going home, then I thought I would stay a bit longer. I must go soon though because I've got work tomorrow.'

'What, you work on a Sunday?' replied Gemma. She was surprised.

'Yes, we 've got to do an extra day tomorrow because they want to trial Sunday opening. It's a one-off, but it's still annoying. If it works out, it might become a regular thing. I'm fed up with my job. I wish I could work for myself. If I had the money to do it, I would,' he explained.

The party had nose-dived. She felt so disappointed by everything. At least Rob was ok because he wasn't trying to impress anyone. She felt surprisingly safe with him because he seemed content to be himself. The more Gemma exchanged conversation with him, the better she felt.

At last, someone accepted her. Trying to impress people was hard, and she was fighting a losing battle competing with Louise! Just how much wine had they gone through, and John had been out to the Off License again to buy yet more wine that nobody wanted as the house was now empty.

Gemma felt her head spin as if she was going to collapse. She suddenly felt embarrassed that she was losing control. If she dropped off to sleep, Louise and John would no doubt end up in the bedroom together.

'I'm going' announced Rob who abruptly moved towards the door. 'Are you coming, Lou?'

Louise didn't reply because she was still in deep conversation! Gemma suddenly thought if Rob left, there would be the three of them and she'd end up being the odd one out!

'No, I'll be along later. It's far too early to leave a party now!' shouted Louise casually.

'That means she won't be home until the morning!' said Rob, looking Gemma straight in the eye. Gemma began to panic, oh no that's terrible, I could be stuck here with them kissing and cuddling all night and I'd have to watch it!

Gemma suddenly decided that her best choice was to go back with Rob because she could always ask him for the taxi fare.

'I'm coming with you,' she said suddenly.

'Ok Gem, but please hurry because I'm not waiting around for anyone. I've got to be up in the morning, and I'm exhausted.' She wondered how she managed to get herself into this situation. She knew part of it was her naivety because she didn't know how any of this worked. She'd been married to Tony for too long! The dating thing had changed since she did it. It seemed as if people didn't bother to go on dates anymore. They just hung around with each other and sex was on offer with no commitment! There seemed to be no expectation of anything. Everything was just a bit of fun, except it wasn't! If she wanted a social life, on a low income, with very few friends, she had to beat them, or join them. However, joining them could expose her to all sorts of behaviours that she didn't want to be involved with. John was one thing, but had she been stupid to trust in him? He could know many women like Louise, and she had been naive. What an idiot she'd been. He was no different than the rest of them!

Gemma walked with Rob to their small, terraced cottage which was fortunately only a few streets away. He walked quickly, and they chatted for a while about the party and a little about Louise.

'The difference between you and Lulu is that you're a grown-up,' said Rob, unexpectedly.

Gemma was surprised to hear him say that because she didn't know that he had an opinion about her. Besides, she knew that he and Louise smoked weed together, so she wondered if that made him withdrawn. He was so numb that he no longer cared about Louise's behaviour.

Rob unlocked the heavy wooden door to their little house. The cottage was tiny, but it had a 'cosy' feel to it. There was a large kitchen with a good range of cupboards, painted in bright fashionable colours. Gemma liked it. There were also houseplants everywhere because Louise was very fond of plants which made it look modern and tasteful. There was a large deep oak table in the centre of the kitchen with some matching chairs, and Rob said she could sit down while he filled the kettle.

'Coffee, lots of it,' he said decisively. We both need to sober up.'

'You'll have to sleep in Lulu's room, ok?' he said, giving Gemma a long look.

Gemma felt relieved because she was drifting off to sleep while sitting up, and all she wanted to do was to go to bed and sleep off the wine. She knew that things wouldn't look so bad in the morning!

The candles flickered wildly. It was a windy night, but Gemma couldn't feel a draught. At least the coffee was giving her time to gather her thoughts. She felt a huge pang of jealousy at the thought of John and Lulu being left alone together but they had left her with little choice. Surely Lulu was trustworthy because they were friends and she knew how she felt. But did anyone understand the depths of Louise's mind? Sometimes she laughed and joked, and Gemma enjoyed her company, but the next time she saw her she'd be met with sarcasm and be pushed away. She was so unpredictable; it made her uneasy. It was possible that Lulu could knock on the door and ask her why she was here with her boyfriend!

But surprisingly, and to Gemma's relief the knock hadn't come, and it was late now.

Gemma began to feel awkward and restless, and wondered whether Rob would lend her the money for a taxi? Staying the night at his house felt like madness. Her and Louise had swapped places! She didn't want to be part of this. Did any of John's friends lead successful lives? Or more to the point, did they have anything to show for their lives! They were the same age as her, but none of them had children. Rob said Lulu couldn't look after children because she couldn't look after herself. He was right. She thought about Johns' children and wondered if they missed their mother. He'd told her that their mother was too busy with her career to see them but was this true? Gemma knew it was not the best idea for her to develop feelings towards his children because John could get into a committed relationship, and it would be hard to break away from them, but she still hoped he wouldn't meet anyone else. She was gutted by the thought of him having sex with different women, but there was nothing she could do about it. If she wanted to remain, friends, she'd have to accept the situation.

Rob told Gemma that he was at the end of the road with Lu and felt their relationship wasn't going to last much longer. While Gemma listened to him talking about it, she began to feel sorry for him. Rob had a busy job as a manager of a computer shop and often worked long hours. He had little support. How many flings had she had? Rob told her that Louise had been unfaithful before and he planned to kick her out. 'It's my house so I can do what I want,' he said angrily.

Gemma wondered if he was strong enough to carry it through. She could see the real Rob was an exhausted weak young man. It would take a lot of courage to stand up to her, more than he had. He suddenly turned to Gemma and told her that he was falling to sleep and needed to go to bed.

'Don't worry about calling a taxi because it's too late now anyway. You can sleep in Louise's room if you like because it doesn't look like she's coming back,' he said. Surprisingly, he didn't appear annoyed. There was a feeling of inevitability about the situation, and he seemed resigned to it.

Gemma climbed the little wooden stairs that led up from the kitchen. It certainly was a quaint little cottage, but it was freezing! They had obviously worked on the place extensively. She wondered if they both did the work or if that was left to Rob?

She entered a charming small bedroom with a single bed and chest of drawers, she suddenly noticed Louise's clothes strewn all over the bed. Scarves, beautiful dresses and blouses, items that she had tried on and discarded so that she could wear the matching red shirt! Gemma sighed. Imagine having the money to buy such beautiful clothes when most of her money was spent on school uniforms. Lu lived in a different world to her. Gemma knew she wasn't part of this frivolous world where clothes, lipstick, drinks, and drugs were commonplace.

It crossed her mind that she'd been out of her depth with John and now she'd put herself into a situation with Rob! What was she doing? Gemma's head felt fuzzy from the wine she'd drank. It was a bad idea to have her secret bottle! When the room started to spin, she quickly removed the items of clothing from the bed and put them on the top of a small pine dressing table. Lu's clothes appeared scrunched, but at least they weren't on the floor. No doubt she'd be annoyed when she discovered her things had been moved and her bed was slept in, but right now there was no other choice.

It was freezing and the bed sheets were ice cold. No doubt, the fire in the kitchen had gone out too, thought Gemma, who had decided that this bedroom was even colder than her own and that was saying something! There were no upstairs heaters, obviously to save costs.

Gemma had never felt this level of loneliness. She wanted to be at home with the girls, snuggled in her own bed. What were her children doing now? Hopefully, they were having fun with their father. Her head had only been on the cold pillowcase for about five minutes when she heard Rob calling to her.

'You can come and give me a cuddle if you like?' he shouted.

'What did you say?' she asked in total disbelief.

Rob repeated it. He was Louise's boyfriend. What was he doing? Gemma was shocked. She knew that Louise was with John, and she was upset about it, but if she slept with Rob, surely it would make things worse. Gemma was confused and at the same time, the sensible part of her thought it was best to let them get on with it! She slowly got out of bed and went to give Rob a cuddle; hoping it would warm her up. As Gemma walked towards Rob's bed, she felt so low. What did she have to lose?

Rob's light was off and he was lying in a large double bed. She thought that he must be out of it after drinking a vast amount of wine. She had no idea how much weed he'd smoked, but the smell wafted around the room and along the landing. It was everywhere and it was horrible. The sweet sickly odour made her feel worse. She climbed into bed next to Rob and snuggled up to him. Rob put his arm around Gemma and drew her close. She gave him a small kiss and quickly pulled away. She lay cuddled up with him for a few minutes, hardly daring to move because it felt so wrong. Gemma then slowly edged her way off the bed and walked towards the door.

'Where are you going?' he asked, sounding surprised.

'I'm going to the other room, to sleep' she replied.

Gemma walked into the little room and climbed into the bed, which had taken a turn for the worse! As her eyes closed, she hoped the morning would come quickly. It seemed incredible that the man she loved was with Louise, and she was sleeping in this cottage with a man who had a drug problem! Worse still, she was still ice cold. Wasn't a party meant to be fun? None of this evening had any element of fun. What a disaster. It suddenly struck her that by being friends with John; she also invited his friends into her life. These people were so different from anyone that she'd met before. They had no responsibilities and did whatever they liked! Rob was right, she was the only grown-up! Children for these people would be a joke when they didn't know the first thing about responsibility. Gemma knew she needed to get her act together and quick. If she didn't, she could soon become one of them, and then, what would happen to Lacey and Lily?

WAKING UP

The sun streamed through the window, and Gemma slowly faced the world! Her nose was frozen, and she could feel a stream of freezing air on her face. She quickly surveyed Louise's clothes which had been piled up on top of the small chest of drawers, and hoped they weren't too crumpled, fearing another drama. She found her own clothes strewn across the bare floorboards and grabbed them quickly so she could leave. There was no sound coming from Rob who was continuing to sleep off a toxic mixture. Gemma then tiptoed down the stairs, not bothering with breakfast or tea and abruptly left. To her surprise, the door was bolted, which meant Louise couldn't have come in even if she'd tried! Gemma quickly undid the locks then stood out in the sunshine. The world looked an entirely different place. It was the small town she recognised instead of her seedy twisted mess of emotions. She had to do something about this now! Her only way forward was to cut herself off from these people, which also meant finishing her friendship with John. Gemma knew it would be hard, but she had to do it, to save herself and her children. She felt a strong urge to speak to him to find out what happened after she left the party last night but decided it was weak. If things became too difficult to stay away, there was always the telephone, but Gemma was going to do her best to keep her distance. It would be easier now she felt angry about Louise. The thought of her and John having sex together made her stomach retch.

Gemma hadn't eaten for hours, and she desperately needed some toast and coffee. Hopefully after that, she'd feel more human. She quickly found her car which was parked outside John's house and drove herself home. She had the rest of the day to pull herself together so she could appear 'normal' when the girls came home early evening. She wanted to be a good parent to the girls and she was determined that from now on her life would be different. She did some tasks around the home and planned to go to bed early because the party had been exhausting. When the girls returned home, they would soon all be back into the familiar routine.

Later, when the children went to bed, Gemma went up as well and decided to put the weekend behind her. It had been a big mistake and one that she'd never repeat. Plus, it had been exhausting, harder work than looking after the girls!

Gemma awoke around 2 am covered in sweat. Her heart was racing. She became aware of a vivid dream which felt more like a visitation. There was a strange mirror, and Gemma felt as though her body had travelled through it and through time. She had stepped to the other side which was an extraordinary experience. But for the first time since her confusion, she'd made a breakthrough. The first thing she noticed was an old woman who was smiling at her, and Gemma quickly became aware that she was standing in a cave. It was dark in the cave, and the woman was pointing to a deep dark well in the corner.

'Don't you remember me, Gemma? You came here when you were ten years old to make a wish. You wished that your mother would be well. She is well now,' said the old woman. Gemma thought hard. Where was she? Was she awake or still in a dream? There was something familiar about the woman who appeared friendly and was trying to tell her something. Gemma realised the woman was telling the truth about her mother. She'd visited the cave with her parents years ago which was a very magical place which stuck in her mind for years. Her mother had suffered from a long-term illness, so she decided to listen.

Gemma had always thought her mother was unwell because there was no cure for her medical condition, and her life had changed in so many ways. Had she been wrong? Was this an illusion? Her mother was happy and made the best of her limitations. She'd recently discovered how to paint, and her oil paintings were incredible. Her mother had her difficulties but had adapted. In a sense, she had found her own magic by exploring her creativity. Gemma suddenly realised that healing was more about working with the soul than the physical body. The woman explained to her that the body was just a vessel, part of our journey, but our soul was eternal. There were many ways to be happy and many reasons to live. Sometimes, people come to terms with their limitations and start to embrace another side of life. Adapting to the restrictions of ill health and moving into acceptance appeared to be part of her mother's healing process.

Gemma looked down into the deep well. The water was black, and it felt as if time had stopped. She stood where she made her wish at ten years old and asked for healing for her mother.

The water dripped from the cave ceiling, then it streamed down Gemma's face, and she fully awoke from her dream. She realised that she'd not been able to see the truth about her mother and so many other things! What she saw was a limited version of the truth, not the whole picture. Images of her life had flashed through the deep dark waters as Gemma experienced her self-created illusions! What had she been doing? Her friends were mirrors reflecting her negative emotions. She had plunged deep into the water into the depths of her being and saw the people around her were merely droplets of water. Her friends had been her teachers, teaching her about herself. Gemma saw it now. She had attracted the wrong people to her because of her negativity. Part of her wanted to stay in the illusion of helplessness and remain a victim. It was more comfortable to blame everything on her circumstances than to take control of her life.

'I can't look any more,' she'd told the woman.

'You know the truth, Gemma. You must learn to listen to your heart. You think the world we live in is real, but most of what we believe is an illusion. Break free now. Go from these people who are tricking and fooling you. They can't give you anything you haven't got already.' The old lady then smiled and disappeared.

This was madness, thought Gemma. Why dream about the cave after all these years. The witch wasn't real. Was she a spirit? Had she been speaking to a spirit? It sounded mad, but then again, in a strange way she felt comforted. It was as if this woman was looking after her? Gemma realised that there were so many things that she didn't know. One of these was earth magic. She felt extraordinary as if she existed in simultaneous dimensions. Her childhood wish had obviously been powerful, and it had worked! She realised that she had spent too much time living in a fantasy and she had to change that and fast!

Gemma felt tired, but she went downstairs to get some breakfast. Had she experienced a dark night of the soul? There were many things, both good and bad which had moved her on a deep level and would be unforgettable. She wanted to tidy the house today and then go for a walk in the wood. The wood was close to her home with an entrance about two hundred metres away. Gemma loved it. When she was anxious or wanted to lose herself, the wood was therapeutic. There were so many different paths, and she was still looking for new ones. There were always unfamiliar places to explore. Sometimes she'd lose her way by taking a wrong turn, but the wood was small, and if she went wrong, invariably she'd come out at a place she recognised. She loved the smell of the pine, the damp earth under her feet, and the bird song. The wood itself was old, but not ancient. She knew that there were other woods which were close by, which dated back to the doomsday book if she wanted to take her car.

Gemma breathed and began to relax. She loved the trees in Eastfield Woods, they made her feel grounded and centred. The woods were full of magic and with her taking regular walks she knew that she'd soon feel energised and happy.

A FRESH START

Gemma was just leaving the supermarket when she bumped into Jo, who she hadn't seen for months. Jo enthusiastically told her that she and a small group of women were learning riding and stable management at a local riding stable, and it was tremendous fun. It took up most of her spare time, so she was sorry she hadn't been in touch for a while!

'You should come too,' Jo said encouragingly. Gemma knew riding was expensive, but she was encouraged by Jo's enthusiasm. There was a tiny amount of money in her savings account which her mother gave her for Christmas, so she could book up a few lessons and see how she got on. It felt the right time to try something different, and she would be in a group who was slightly ahead of her, which would be useful.

Tuesday morning quickly came, and the sun shone through the clouds. It still felt like winter because it was cold, but it was now late March, and the crocuses were peeping through the damp earth.

The children were both at school today, and Gemma had things organised, so she had the day free to do as she pleased. She felt cold and quickly put some logs on the fire before it went out. Gemma hoped the fire would smoulder until her return, so it didn't have to be re-lit. Riding could be the thing she had been looking for. A new challenge and a chance to meet new people. Her lesson was at the same time as Jo's, so it was going to be fun!

It was ten o'clock, and Gemma stood in some borrowed riding boots looking dismayed. She had forgotten how big horses were, because it had been years since she'd been on a horse. Gemma remembered that years ago when she was on holiday with her parents in Wales, she went trekking on a small pony. Gemma and her sister had their ponies led along a country lane because neither of them could ride. For her first lesson, her horse was also going to be led around the ring, but at least she would learn the basics. Over the next few weeks, they would learn to trot, and sometime later they would start to canter!

Lynne, who was one of the teachers at the stables, smiled at Gemma. 'Your horse is called Whisper, and he's not that big,' she said encouragingly.

'But I can't get up. I've tried over and over, and I'm not strong enough to pull myself all the way up there!' Gemma replied.

'No worries, beginners use the mounting block,' replied Lynne as she led the horse over to the block. Gemma walked over to mount Whisper and managed it quickly. Despite his size, it didn't look as high sitting on Whisper as it appeared from the ground, but she still felt a little shaky.

Jo waited patiently for her on her mare. She had a 'pony on loan' called Flyer and Flyer could do just that, fly. He could take off at any time, and he needed someone dependable to take control, but Jo had always enjoyed a challenge. She had already finished learning with the beginners' ponies, and she now wanted one that was a bit more forward going because she was jumping. Jo said Flyer was chestnut, and Whisper piebald but Gemma didn't know a lot about horse breeds but she had noticed the horses at the stables were well-groomed. Lynne told them that they were brushed every day, and a farrier shoed them regularly.

'Jo, you take the lead with Flyer while we go around the ring a few times, then you can go into the sand school and do some jumping with Jenny, while I continue with Gemma.'

Jo nodded her head. She was wearing a black riding hat, tight black britches, long riding boots and a back protector. Gemma couldn't believe how smart her friend looked in jodhpurs, when she was wearing a pair of second-hand riding boots and a little button-up jacket that she had owned for years. Jo explained it wasn't necessary to buy riding gear unless you had regular lessons because it was expensive.

As Whisper approached the ring, he started to walk a little faster and broke into a trot.

'Good boy Whisper. He loves a little trot around in the mornings; he's such a good horse for starters,' Lynne said.

Gemma thought they were walking, but she began to relax and moved her body in time with the horse. It felt as if she was starting to bond with Whisper already. It gave her a feeling of both anticipation and excitement, which was something she hadn't experienced for a long time. They did three circuits of the ring where Lynne led Whisper and Gemma started to enjoy herself.

'Gemma, I am going to teach you a little sitting trot because Jo's been doing this for several weeks. It's early for you to start, but your balance is perfect, so I'm sure you will get on fine. If you want to stop, just let me know, and we can let Jo continue. Now Gemma, what I want you to do, is to hold the reins while you hold on to the saddle.' Lynne explained.

Gemma was worried she'd fall, but Lynne continued, 'I want you to hold on with your legs and sink deeply into the saddle because this will improve the way you ride.' Gemma grabbed hold of the front of the saddle, feeling worried that she would fall off. She was scared, and at the same time, she was excited. Her feet were out of the stirrups, and her legs clung to the horse's sides.

Gemma started to bounce in the saddle, but she remembered to hold on to the front of it and to keep her legs long. After a while, her body sunk into the saddle and began to go with the horse's movement. It was extraordinarily bumpy, and Gemma was surprised that she didn't slip sideways, but she found that she moved well with Whisper. Gemma was enjoying herself but realised that she might be aching all over tomorrow because she was using muscles that she hadn't used for years.

'Alright, that's enough now,' called Lynne and Whisper slowed down. Then Lynne suggested that

Gemma learned rising trot. Gemma was surprised this was a lot easier than sitting trot. It was difficult getting the rhythm at first, but when she did, it was great fun.

Jo had left the ring, and Gemma noticed that she was in the sand ring, cantering. Gemma was amazed because Jo had only been riding for about six months, and she was cantering already! Gemma had no idea you could learn to ride this quickly although riding already felt natural to her and she felt she'd be good at it. Thank goodness she'd found something to put her energies into, which was positive and rewarding. At least it was a step in the right direction.

HEALING

Gemma's hands were hot again, and she didn't know why. She wondered where all the heat was coming from. If one of her children had a headache or felt unwell, her hands were instantly hot. In addition to this strange experience, Gemma kept having distant memories about an old couple that she'd listened to as a teenager while waiting for the bus.

It had been a way of passing the time. They always sounded so interesting but she'd never understood what it was all about. The couple always talked about the cards. If something was in the cards, from what Gemma gathered, it was a good thing, and if it wasn't showing up in the cards, then it was unlikely to happen! This puzzled Gemma, but she never discussed it with anyone because it was eavesdropping, and she was embarrassed by it. It had made the time go more quickly especially on a cold or wet day! The couple regularly appeared in all weathers and she often wondered where they lived. Why did they say these things when other people could hear them? They seemed incredibly open about their messages and it didn't appear to bother them that they were overheard!

Gemma found it intriguing. She'd often wondered what these cards were, then someone told her they sounded like Tarot cards, which were fortune-telling cards that had been around for years. Gemma was fascinated and this made sense to her. The elderly couple must use tarot cards. Her friend said it was possible to find out many things from them if you know how to use them, including the past and the future, but they had to be treated with respect because they were powerful. Gemma quickly realised the tarot wasn't a game; and these things said at the bus stop were serious business!

Gemma's first intuitive experience happened at the age of eight when her cat died and it still made her sad if she thought about it. It was a terrible thing because he was only eleven months old. Sadly, Timmy got run over by a car because they lived on an extremely busy road. However, the night before he was run down by a car, Gemma knew that something was going to happen to him, and she said goodbye to her cat. Tears ran down her face because she knew it would be the last time that she'd see him, so they said goodbye. When the next day came and her mother shouted to her to come and say farewell to Timmy because he had been hit by a car, Gemma was so upset that she shut her bedroom door in horror. It appeared that not only did she know her cat was about to leave this world, but she knew about it well before anyone else! Gemma didn't want this thing, whatever it was because it didn't always bring good news, but she had little choice.

'Gemma,' she heard a voice calling her and swung around to see who it was, but there was no-one there. It had happened many times since she was a child, and it still did on odd occasions. She wished she knew where the voice came from. If there was a person around to help, it was a good thing, and she wouldn't be frightened. It could be her Guardian Angel trying to communicate with her. That was a comforting thought and she decided not to worry about being called. There was obviously a reason for it, and for now she had to accept that she didn't know what it was.

* * * * * * *

It was a cold winter's evening, and Gemma had started the fire. It felt like an old friend. Her other friends were the trees in the wood which showed their tops over her fence, which was a constant reminder of their presence. She thought for a moment it was strange to befriend trees and then later burn them! Yet, it was symbolic of how nature serves human beings, and it was necessary. Gemma knew she could always rely on Mother Nature when she started to doubt herself. She often thought if someone was listening to her, the earth was, and it uplifted her. She was frustrated because she found that despite everything that had happened, she was still spending too much time thinking about John. She hadn't seen him since the party and started to wonder if he was with anyone. Did he miss her or think about her?

When Gemma arrived home from her riding lesson, she looked for her tarot cards. She had three books on the tarot and a pack of cards, called Ryder Waite which were given to her by Tony's mother. His mother used the cards many years ago and had tried to learn their meanings. The cards were still in their original packaging and wrapped in a square of dark blue velvet. She put them on one side. She'd use them another day because she was going to visit a friend this evening who held a meditation group in High Wycombe. It was a long drive, but she considered it worth the trip because they always had such great discussions which often went on into the early hours of the morning. Although it was hard for Gemma to travel to all the meetings, she usually met the ladies once a month and organised a sitter for the girls.

The group had great fun at each other's houses. They talked about meditation and discussed each other's experiences. One of the ladies Helga was learning something called Reiki which was an ancient healing system. She was told that you went through various stages called degrees. There were three in all. She listened to Helga for ages because this fascinated her. Gemma wondered if it was something she could do in the future. She explained about her hands becoming hot to Helga. 'Yes, that's what happens when you have the Reiki attunement. It means that you are open to receiving healing energy. When you take the first Reiki Degree, you will see how different it feels. It can feel as if your hands are on fire!' explained Helga.

Gemma listened to her story which sounded amazing! Her friend had already started healing people and was experiencing excellent results. One of the members of the group called Susan, said that she'd hold the next meeting at her house. She lived in a town about twelve miles away, which was great for Gemma because it was nearer than High Wycombe. Susan had arranged for them all to have a short reading with a man called Frank, who was terrific at tarot readings and had agreed to give everyone a quick reading.

Gemma called the mother of the twins who lived at the bottom of the hill. Usually, one or the other of them would be free to stay with the girls the evening. She told the girls that the twins were coming and tried to explain which twin would babysit to Lacey and Lily, but most of the time, she didn't know herself! Lacey told Gemma how to identify the twins and said that they knew the difference. Gemma laughed. Her children were amazing!

Susan lived in a lovely house which was set back from the road with a beautiful front garden full of flowers in nearby Abington. It was a very peaceful setting with trees in the front garden where the birds sang their hearts out. Susan said that she'd been living there for quite a few years. Her children were the same age as Lacey and Lily, but she had boys who were a bit of a handful. Susan said they were always good when people came to visit! She told them that her husband was supportive because they shared the chores and looked after the children between them. She was presently attending a training course in London, so most of her days were full. The boys had gone to bed, but you could still hear light footsteps on the landing. Eventually, around 9 pm, there was silence, and the group started the evening with meditation while they waited for Frank's arrival.

It was beginning to get late and everyone had seen Frank except Gemma who realised she was last. Susan told them that he was an excellent reader, and she wouldn't be disappointed and not to worry because he wouldn't cut her reading short. The girls had gone in one at a time and they were gone for twenty minutes. Each person was seen on their own for privacy, and it was working well.

Gemma was feeling tired. It was quickly approaching nine-thirty, and Susan told her that he wouldn't be much longer. Frank was magical and wise, and he also knew the mysteries of life. Gemma knew that she needed a little direction, so she thought it would be a chance for her to learn more about herself. If she had enough time, she'd mention to him about the strange experiences she had with the woman in the cave and even about her hands becoming hot. But the thing Gemma wanted to know about the most was John, was she ever going to be with him.

When at last she heard Frank's voice through the door, she realised that he sounded familiar. It was strange, but for a few seconds she was fifteen years old. As the elderly man walked towards her with a kind and sincere face, she smiled.

'Come on in Gemma,' Frank announced, as if he was expecting her.

Gemma took a long deep breath. She couldn't believe it; Frank was the gentleman from the bus stop. He had talked about the cards whenever she caught the bus to town. And now the same man was here in front of her. Should she tell him? Was it rude to say that she had met him before. Could it change the dynamic of the reading? She suddenly felt quite embarrassed and wanted to slip away.

'I'm sorry for keeping you waiting. I know it's been a long evening, but I wanted you to come in last so that I can have a little longer with you. Frank then sat down with Gemma at a small table and began to spread out the cards. You have all the major arcana here,' he said.

'What does that mean?' asked Gemma wanting to know if that was in any way significant.

'It says that you will be doing the same kind of work as me. Spiritual work and you will also teach. You need to keep moving in a spiritual direction because you have a gift. You must use that gift but never forget about the sun because the sun is an ancient Egyptian symbol, and it holds so much power. Learn to trust and follow your intuition. Follow the sun, and you won't go far wrong. That's the outcome, and it's good,' said Frank.

Gemma looked at the cards. She'd never encountered magic like this before! The pictures on the tarot cards told a story which drew her like a magnet. She wanted to pick up Frank's cards because they were terrific. She decided to take the plunge and tell him that they had met before.

'I've seen you and your wife before. It was years ago when I was a teenager. I used to listen to you talking about the cards at the bus stop,' she blurted.

'Yes, I remember you, but you didn't have to worry because the other people couldn't hear us. You only heard us because you were supposed to. It may have appeared we were talking loudly, but we weren't. Most people didn't know we were there,' Frank explained.

'You mean you were invisible to them?' Gemma answered, finding it hard to understand what he was saying.

'Yes, invisible to many people, apart from those who were meant to hear us! Keep walking towards the sun, and one day you will understand,' he repeated. Gemma felt slightly bewildered, but she was also happy and fascinated.

'I also knew you in ancient Egypt,' continued Frank. Gemma wasn't sure what to say. Frank felt familiar as if they knew each other. Anything was possible she thought. There were obviously a lot of things she had to learn.

'Thank you,' she said, then realised that she hadn't asked anything about John!

When she returned to the other room, the girls asked her what Frank had said, but she found it hard to put into words. What had taken place? It was undoubtedly 'a reading,' but there were no words to say how it made her feel. It was like the experience she had in the cave. It felt as if past, present, and future were overlapping in the same space. She quickly checked to see if she still had two feet on the ground, thankfully she had. For a while she felt strange. She didn't know Frank, but she felt an instant affinity with him. The others in the group said it was a connection. Gemma felt puzzled. It was all very well talking about all this hocus pocus stuff, but she had to go home and wash the girls' school uniforms, before she went to bed. It was getting late, and she needed to get going. Motivating the girls wasn't easy at the best of times, especially not in the winter because they didn't like getting out of bed.

Gemma felt a little disappointed that she hadn't asked about John. Still, she had her own cards so she could find out for herself. It would be easy to practice reading them with the help of the books because the books had been labelled. Surely it wasn't that hard? Whatever happened, she wasn't going to be governed by them! She didn't want to put her life into the hands of destiny. She preferred to have free will and power over her own life. She had spent years agreeing with Tony at every point in their relationship because if not, he sulked then lost his temper. Accepting what he said had become her only choice even if it made her unhappy. If his shirts weren't ironed and ready for him, he would say 'where's my shirt?' If she forgot for some reason, he would give her a tough time. She felt that it was her duty as a wife to look after him, but it wasn't the relationship she wanted. Gemma wanted someone to care about her. Tony seldom showed her that he cared, which eventually led to her feelings of isolation and loneliness.

Gemma missed her early life working in a Bank because she was good with figures and had an alert mind. Although she dearly loved Lacey and Lily, she felt a need for some adult company because her days revolved around school trips, housework and getting meals ready. Sometimes there was a little social interaction with other mums from the school, such as an occasional coffee or the odd pub lunch together but that was rare. She had skills she could use, and the money would be useful. She could meet her own needs and pay for extra activities for the girls. None of that had been possible in her relationship with Tony, and she didn't regret getting out of that situation. She couldn't bear the fact that she was not allowed or encouraged to contribute to family life. Gemma had been squashed into a box she no longer fitted. Deep inside her was a suppressed free spirit. But now she had her freedom, what could she do with it? Having freedom was exciting, but it wasn't a straightforward process because she'd met Tony at such an early age, and she hadn't learned independence. She had always shared a room with her sisters and didn't remember a time when she had her 'own space.' Nor was she completely free to make her own decisions until now. It felt like the right time to get a job. Her cottage was decorated in the way that she wanted. She could travel at the weekends while Tony looked after the girls. It was amazing to have this newfound freedom, and she could feel it rising inside her. She smiled. It was scary, but it was also exciting. The excitement was something she rarely felt apart from when John was close. He had looked at her in a questioning way as he tried to fathom her deeper levels. She loved to look into his dark piercing eyes and to think I know you. I know your soul. Gemma knew it was love, but it wasn't returned.

Funding her riding lessons was challenging which made Gemma more determined to find a job. She loved riding Whisper and wanted to carry on. If she gave up horse riding, she'd be miserable! Gemma turned over the page in the paper and suddenly saw an advertisement which looked interesting.

Part-time waiter/server needed in a busy local coffee shop in Witney. Afternoons only. Hours by arrangement.

Afternoons would be great for her. It would give her time to do housework in the mornings and go for a riding lesson. She could pick up the children after three. If she got an interview, she could do twelve to four pm rather than one to four which would fit in even better.

Margery picked up the telephone. She'd received many phone calls, but this girl Gemma could start at short notice, so she decided to offer her a brief interview. Margery took to Gemma at once. Gemma appeared approachable and friendly and had an 'openness' which would be an asset with her customers.

The café was modern and slightly 'hip,' and as Margery didn't want to employ anyone stuffy Gemma seemed perfect. The girl also looked fit, which was another asset because the floor needed to be swept and washed daily. The job was quite physical compared to office work, but Gemma had the right attitude and a reference from a cleaning job. She'd also explained that she was handy with a saw and didn't appear afraid of arduous work which went down well. Margery decided to give her the job on the spot! The shop was already busy, and on Saturdays it was a madhouse, so the sooner Gemma started the better!

GEMMA'S FIRST DAY

Gemma wasn't sure how she'd got the job in the cafe, but she was thrilled. It wasn't perfect because the pay was less than she wanted, but she thought it would do for now and it would be a new challenge. It fitted in well with school hours, which was her primary concern. It was quite different from her professional work in the bank, but it was a fresh start and the past had gone! The job would bring in a small income, and with her allowances as a single parent she could manage.

Serving the customers was fun. Gemma loved meeting people, so she knew she'd enjoy the job. Everything would have to be written down, so she didn't forget anything. Margery, the owner of the cafe, told her not to worry and assured her that everything would come in time. All in good time, thought Gemma who knew that she had to calm down and slow down! The cafe was packed with people at lunch time, which made the time go exceptionally fast, and by two forty, Gemma was wiping the furniture, sweeping then mopping the floor. Then she'd fly off to collect her daughters.

The girls were now at the same school in town, which was only five minutes' drive from the café. Although Gemma was often tired when she left, she'd soon recover at the sight of her daughters. Lacey was now ten and in the top year, and Lily was eight, a couple of school years behind her. They both loved school, and they were doing well. There were the occasional moans about not wanting to go, but usually it wasn't a problem. Her girls often got ready in their smart skirts and blouses and just got on with it, which made things easier. The girls were growing up extremely fast, especially Lacey, who at ten years old was only about six inches smaller than her and had started to look like a teenager! Her hair and olive complexion were often mistaken for her being Spanish or Italian which Lacey found amusing. Where she got her looks from Gemma didn't know, but when the sun came out her skin quickly turned dark. Her great grandfather was Italian, but their family history was a little vague.

It was a beautiful day with the sun shining, and the grass had grown long at the front of the cottage. At the weekend Gemma planned to cut it and tidy up the flower borders. They now had some electric heaters in the house due to her continually nagging the landlord. This was fantastic and really took the edge off the last few winter months. Fortunately, it was now spring, and there was no need for Gemma to have the heating or the fire on unless it was an unusually cold evening. Those evenings were now less frequent because it was the end of April, and flowers were blooming everywhere. The daffodils were over, and roses had come into bud while the blackbirds sang!

Gemma weakened and telephoned John to see how he was. He seemed happy to hear from her and suggested that she pop round for a coffee on Saturday.

He told Gemma that he was now dating his former boss and that he'd started a new job for a large software company in Bicester. It was a lot of travelling, but the money was good, and he said he was enjoying it. Gemma wasn't an expert at the cards, but she'd already seen this woman appear in her spreads and she guessed that John had met someone. It was a spontaneous decision to have a quick coffee with him after she'd finished gardening because on Sunday, she planned to go to a mind body and soul exhibition. Gemma was extremely excited by the thought of meeting some like-minded people. The other ladies from the meditation group had also said that they might pop in, but Gemma decided that to explore it properly she'd need to go on her own. It would be tempting to have a reading because it had been a while since she had the one with Frank. She was unsure where Frank did his readings. There was a possibility that he could also be at the exhibition so there may be some faces she recognised.

The weekend arrived quickly, and her daughters had already packed their bags with schoolbooks, pencil cases and textbooks as well as clothes, which astounded Gemma. They were getting so independent at times. It was amazing how quickly this happened, but it allowed Gemma to get her own things organised. She was really looking forward to meeting up with John for a quick catch up and she wondered if his relationship with his work colleague had turned into something serious.

John had been sitting in the kitchen, sipping coffee while eating biscuits and he brought Gemma into the kitchen so she could join him. This was something he always did on a Saturday. They sat together and talked about their children for a while. His children were not there this weekend because they were with their mother, so they could catch up. As John spoke, Gemma noticed that he seemed a completely different person! He wasn't interested in anything she had to say and he certainly didn't appear to have missed her. He was still keen to tell her that he managed to seduce Emily after they had been out on a date. The connection had soon turned into a sexual relationship which had been going on for several months, which also included having sex in the office, which he found exciting.

Gemma fought to bite back the tears. She couldn't believe how flippant he was. His entire conversation was about the challenge of seducing this woman and the rewards that went with it! She felt both jealous and angry and wondered if he planned on taking their relationship to the next level. He kept saying that he knew it wouldn't last, but Gemma wasn't convinced. Why bother with it at all then, Gemma thought angrily. Once again, she reminded herself that they were just friends, and even though they had shared some intimate moments there hadn't been any promises. It felt like torture, but part of her knew that it was her own fault for imagining their friendship was turning into something more. She wondered how two people could be so intimate and it meant nothing. Her heart sank, and she felt fearful.

Gemma decided to rush to the toilet to tidy her hair and apply more makeup. When she'd fixed her eyes and reapplied her lipstick, she decided to put on a brave face.

Her short skirt and long-sleeved top with a scooped neck made her look slim, and she liked her appearance today. But whatever effort she made for John, she never felt good enough. What was he looking for? Whatever it was, it wasn't her. She was too deep a person for him and took life seriously, and he was flippant. Today it was hard for her to meet him on any level at all. He no longer wanted to talk about his children or anything that had originally drawn them together. When they first met, he'd been interested in spirituality but that had been completely forgotten!

'I'm going now John,' she said at last.

'Oh, you're off already. Okay, but do you have to leave just yet because I wanted to show you some photographs I took when I went away with the children last weekend,' he asked, as he went to re boil the kettle.

Gemma's throat felt stuck. She wanted to leave. If she stayed any longer, she'd burst into tears and things could quickly become awkward.

'I really do have to go now John because I'm decorating the girl's bedrooms. I want to try and get at least one room finished before they get back tomorrow evening,' she said, hoping that he wouldn't realise the real reason for her hasty departure.

'Ok, but if you want to come back later, I have a few people here for drinks tonight,' he said trying to get her attention.

Gemma turned to go, then she decided to stay a little longer and tried her best to appear casual, despite being a quivering wreck. The image of the slim dark-haired woman stuck in her mind as her imagination dressed her in a smart business suit, sophisticated blouse, and elegant heels. The woman was no doubt an excellent manager! Although computer software sounded extremely dull, it had obviously impressed John. Gemma knew they were no longer the same people. We connected for a while, and now we're walking two quite different paths, she thought. It had become obvious to her that John was being drawn into the business world, and her world, was spiritual. If we ever come back together in the future, we do, but it's certainly not now, she thought with newfound clarity.

Gemma got in her car to drive back home to the peace of her cottage and the familiar trees. The deep pink paint awaited her. It was a great colour to paint Lacey's bedroom, and she suddenly felt quite excited. She'll love it, she thought. No, we will love it. Lily will love it too. She quickly lifted the lid of the large plastic tub and stirred. The colour swirled around for a few moments before it took on a slightly different shade. Paint often took on a different tone when it was mixed, she thought putting a splodge on the wall. The old beige colour on the walls was a little flaky, but she decided to paint over the top as there wasn't the time to do anything else. Gemma marvelled at how the deep pink made the walls spring to life. The colour totally lifted her heart, and she couldn't wait for her girls to return and see the transformation! Decorating was Gemma's way of healing a broken heart, and it worked wonders!

SUNDAY

Gemma walked around the large hall. She was fascinated by the smiling people, and the brightly coloured clothes they were wearing. The combination of the smells and the relaxing spiritual music was intoxicating, and she was in a haze which lifted her emotionally, but she also felt floaty! She noticed a good-looking older man playing the didgeridoo, and slowly walked over to watch him.

'Would you like a go?' asked the man as he handed the long wooden instrument to Gemma. Surprisingly, the didge was extremely heavy, being made from wood. She tried to blow into the top of it to make a noise, but it was impossible. Nothing came out!

Gemma felt feeble and slightly embarrassed by her attempts, but the man looked at her and smiled. He told her there was a 'knack' to it! Gemma thought this was one thing she was never going to be able to do and so she walked on, thinking there would be another opportunity in the future. The sound that came from the instrument was beautiful, but she concluded that it was best left to the experts!

Gemma worked her way slowly around the stands and into another hall and continued to look at the incredible stalls. She spent a long time in front of the crystal stall because Lily had asked if she could bring back a crystal. There were many unusual types of stones that she didn't know the names of which were vibrant. Some of them produced the most incredible light. If she took one home for Lily, then Lacey could be upset, and Gemma always tried to treat them equally, so she decided to look for two gifts. She picked up a piece of heart-shaped rose quartz and held it in her hand for a few minutes trying to sense if it was right for her daughter. While she was deciding, she glanced around the room and noticed a handsome man about the same age as herself sitting about five metres away in the corner of the café. He was on his own and appeared to be drinking coffee. Gemma felt an instant attraction to him. He was exceptionally good looking. He appeared Italian and had black shoulder length hair. The man was neither slim nor broad and he wore a purple tee shirt with a spiral pattern on the front which reminded her of a musical note. Was it a reiki symbol? He suddenly noticed Gemma looking across at him and he smiled, holding her gaze for a few minutes. Gemma wondered what he was doing at the exhibition and if he was still working. He then glanced at his watch, stood up and strolled towards a table at the rear of the hall. He was giving a reading, and he had a pack of tarot cards which were spread on the table, along with some beautiful crystals. As Gemma moved closer, she noticed an astrology chart was open on his laptop. Gemma wanted to talk to the man but decided to get a coffee instead because it was now late afternoon, and the café would close soon. She was surprised how fast the time had flown while she was browsing. Thankfully, there were no worries about her getting back to the children today because Tony had them. It felt like bliss to have an entire day to herself and to be able to wander as slowly as she liked without continual clock watching.

Gemma finished her coffee and cake and went to see what the man was doing. She didn't want to appear too obvious because their eyes had already met, but Gemma's curiosity had got the better of her! Alessandro looked busy, and as she approached his table, the candles flickered wildly, and she looked up. Gemma noticed a midnight blue cloth, along with an ancient set of tarot cards with incredible images. There were also three books on astrology and a laptop, which Alessandro obviously used for his charts. The candles continued to flicker erratically, and Gemma wondered where the breeze was coming from. She decided to step back slightly because they might blow out. She realised the lady who sat opposite him was only at the start of her reading and it would be unfair to invade her privacy. She also noticed there was a large piece of rose quartz and a crystal ball on a silver stand which looked ancient, and besides that, there was a waiting list. She picked up a leaflet from his table which read 'Alessandro, Astrologer and Tarot Reader. Having an astrology forecast is a unique experience which enables you to release the past by unleashing your full potential. With the aid of the tarot, you can have a better insight into career, health, and relationships.' Gemma smiled. She liked the wording, and decided to have a reading with Alessandro because his leaflet was excellent, and he appeared very professional. There was a lengthy list of names. He was booked until four forty-five, then there was a line which showed her that he intended to finish at that point. She turned to talk to the man at the next table.

'He looks busy. Do you know if he's any good?' she asked.

'You'll be lucky if you get in with him today,' replied the man. Gemma noticed that this poor gentleman didn't appear busy at all despite having a lovely stand. She felt slightly sorry for him. He was selling a variety of items, from silver jewellery to bandanas, which made her think he had a shop. Then she noticed the name of his shop artistically written on a large banner to the back of him. She couldn't quite read it because it was too high up but there was no doubt that it could be seen from the entrance of the hall.

'Is he any good?' repeated Gemma.

'Yes, I believe so because he's always got a queue of women and a few men! He draws people like a magnet. I've been dead quiet all afternoon, and I travelled all the way from London. I'm beginning to think today was a waste of time,' he replied looking upset.

Gemma thought he appeared downhearted.

'Well, I'd love to book a reading with him, but he's full until four forty-five. I really need to be off by then,' she said.

'Oh, so you're in a hurry, are you?' he answered with a grin! There's no time like the present. Did you know the present is a gift?' he said, suddenly perking up then gave her a smile.

Gemma thought for a moment. He was right, what was the hurry? It was madness. She had no-one to rush home to, so there was plenty of time. She realised it was hard to be in the present when she was always rushing. She spent too much time worrying about her future when it was unnecessary, and now it was time to look after her! With this, she boldly walked up to Alessandro's table, picked up the pen, crossed through the line and put her name down. Well, if he's done that many, one more shouldn't be a problem, she thought confidently!

Half an hour later, Alessandro looked into Gemma's eyes. He obviously doesn't have a fear of eye contact, she thought as she stared back at him.

'Right then Gemma, I don't know why I have you because I had put a line to say that I'm finished, but now you are here, shall we have a look at what is coming up?' asked Alessandro, whose tone appeared a little severe.

He started by asking her date and time of birth, then put her details into his laptop. He also asked her to take three tarot cards. He was silent for a few moments, then he started to jot down some information on a note pad. Gemma waited for him to speak without interrupting, which she found difficult!

'Gemma, what I can see for you, is that you need to be alone. You may not like it because at times you will feel quite lonely, but it's not the right time for you to have a relationship. It would be unwise for you to get into anything serious. I can see there's been a recent disappointment and another one a few years ago. The big one, caused you to completely change your life. Right now, you're feeling a little let down. Don't worry, this won't last because you'll discover your path and learn to take control of situations more easily.' said Alessandro, as he glanced at his laptop.

'Yes, you're right. I've been badly let down. There have been a lot of disappointments but what I wanted to know about was my friendship with a man who lives near me. He has two children. Will we become a couple in the future. Does he love me? I have a feeling that deep down he does,' she continued hardly pausing for breath.

'Love, I can't see love for you any time soon. I'm sorry to say there's a disappointment here. Something you wished for doesn't work out the way you want. Love is such a funny word. There are many types of love. I can also see a short relationship coming up for you soon. It won't last, but while it does it will be exciting!' replied Alessandro, confidently.

'Exciting, thought Gemma, what's that? Can relationships be exciting? Surely good relationships were about stability and love, then eventually settling down. What Alessandro said, really surprised her. She knew it would cause her to think hard. Exciting was exciting though, wasn't it? Did there have to be a reason for it? Surely there didn't have to be a reason for everything! Sometimes she hated the whole prediction thing. She didn't want to take everything so seriously, and she needed to find her flow. Life was confusing. If she put her faith in the cards, was she still making her own decisions? She was beginning to feel a little lost. Why did she waste her time listening to Frank and his wife at the bus stop? This was where it had all started many years ago. How could it be exciting waiting for a bus? Her mind began to wander, and she suddenly heard Alessandro cough loudly.'

'Do you want me to continue?' he said, looking slightly agitated. Gemma suddenly noticed the clock on the wall which said five o'clock. She had already had fifteen minutes and there were only five minutes left!

'Yes please, sorry. It's just that I don't have that much experience of relationships because I met my husband Tony years ago when we were young. There haven't really been in others. I'm not sure I like being divorced. Sometimes I love it, and other times I hate being on my own,' she blurted. Gemma was a little annoyed that she'd revealed so much personal information. It was embarrassing. She looked across at Alessandro, but he was in a world of his own. He was fixed on bringing information through. He was noting down the relationships between different planets while looking in a book. He also had four tarot cards out in front of him, Ten of Swords, Two of Cups, Queen of Swords then Justice. Alessandro sensed Gemma's disappointment with his reading.

'You'll always be friends with this man, but there's a lesson in it for you. It's a past life relationship, a karmic thing. It would certainly appear that way in your chart. There may be a few more of them by the looks of things.' he continued.

Gemma sighed deeply and tried to hide her emotions, but she felt like crying. Other relationships were irrelevant because she only wanted to know about

John. The past life information was confusing, and it felt as if her head had been bashed against a wall because there were no definite answers. Her friends had told her to give up on him, and she was aware that she'd stopped listening to herself. She was stuck! For goodness sake. She'd even had a visitation from a witch! How much more evidence did she need? There was a new path for her now, and she needed to let go of John completely. The reading had confirmed that they were no longer walking in the same direction, whatever that direction was? That was something she was yet to discover, but right now, exciting sounded good. Maybe if she went with that feeling, things would feel better.

'Call me, and we can talk about it more. I must go now because I've got to pack up, plus I have a long journey home. If you'd like a longer reading, my number is on there. I can make us some lunch.' Alessandro said abruptly while handing her his leaflet. Gemma didn't reply. If she was honest, she was a little shocked. It was strange that Alessandro would invite her to lunch! Was it the continuation of her reading, or a date? Whatever it was, it was unexpected. She then smiled at him in acknowledgement. His eyes were menacing yet compelling, and his Italian accent heightened his charm. How can I be devastated by one man and attracted to another, she thought. It was madness! Gemma suddenly realised there were many words to understand and exciting was one of them.

THE FOLLOWING WEEK

Gemma dialled the phone number that Alessandro gave to her at the event. It was the afternoon, the girls were at school, and she had the day off work. She was excited about the possibility of going to see Alessandro in Oxford and she hoped that he would remember her from all the women at the event.

'Hello Alessandro, it's Gemma. I met you at the event on Saturday,' she said nervously. Her nerves caused her to mumble!

'Hello Gemma, yes of course I remember you, don't be silly! We shall meet to finish the reading and have lunch. How about ... Tuesday,' he asked. Gemma was once again in awe of Alessandro's accent which sounded so charming that for a few minutes she was lost with what to say. Tuesday, that's tomorrow, or did he mean next Tuesday? Her heart began to race, and she felt like her mouth was dry.

'Do you mean tomorrow?' she finally managed to say wondering if that was even possible!

'Yes, I mean tomorrow. I will give you directions and you can come to my house. It will only take you about an hour to drive, and we can finish your chart,' he continued.

Gemma was unsure. She had felt an instant attraction to him, but she didn't know him, and he wanted her to stay for lunch. It was a lovely idea especially as he mentioned that they could have a barbeque. Alessandro had a good reputation as an astrologer, but would she be safe on her own with him in his house? There was no-one to ask, so she tried to tune into her gut feeling. Gemma usually trusted her instinct, and she was frequently right, but it was neither yes nor no. She had to admit that for the first time in years she felt excited. It would be fun finding his house, having the reading, and getting to know him a little more over lunch. He must like me, she thought, to go to the trouble of lunch when he could just finish the chart. It looked as if they were going to be special friends, she thought as a thrill ran through her body.

'Yes, that's great Alessandro. I'll see you tomorrow around twelve,' she found herself saying.

The next day Gemma eagerly put on a short orange cotton dress. She looked in the mirror. The dress set off her beautiful skin and hair. She looked gorgeous. For the first time in ages she didn't feel like a slob. Someone had looked at her as if she was a woman. Not a mother, or a mate, but a woman and she liked it. She noticed that over the past few weeks her body had become toned and shapely. It must have been sawing logs for the fire over the last few months and all the challenging work at the cafe. Now spring was here. The sun was out, and it was time for her to go exploring. She decided to blow with the wind for a while and see where life took her. The fool appeared. Surely that was positive!

THE MEETING

Gemma drove for what felt like hours, although she had calculated that the trip to Oxford was just over an hour. She felt like an excited child, and although she knew her heart was still with John, at least she was trying to get to know other men. She was unsure whether Alessandro regarded it as a lunch date, or work. He'd told her on the phone that he often invited women he met at events, to his home. Even so, she couldn't wait to see him, although there was little doubt, that he could easily charm her! She pulled up outside a detached house on the outskirts of Oxford. The house was in a cheerful avenue with trees on either side. It was situated not too far from the main road, so she found it quickly.

The sun was out, and it looked like an excellent day for a barbeque. Alessandro had said on the telephone that he wouldn't start the lunch until she arrived because he wanted to finish the reading first. Gemma thought that it might be hours before they ate. She was already hungry and a little concerned because she'd have to leave at four o'clock. Her friend Anna was going to pick up the girls tonight, but she needed to be back by five-thirty. She nervously rang the doorbell and stood back but her heart was pounding. It reminded Gemma of the feelings she experienced when visiting John!

Alessandro arrived at his door in a pair of tight jeans, and a white cotton shirt which emphasised his dark Italian looks and his eyes twinkled. Gemma looked down. She found it embarrassing to stare too deeply into his eyes. He was captivating, but part of her was also slightly scared that he might notice her undeniable attraction.

'Hello Gemma, well you got here quickly. I wasn't expecting you for another half an hour or so, but that's good. We can do the chart and then we can get going with the barbeque. It will take a while because I must clean the grills. They are still dirty from my last one. I've been away, so I have had no time to do anything lately! Gemma tried not to appear anxious, but she knew she was nervous. It seemed rude when Alessandro was making lunch to keep on about the time so she decided to relax and enjoy herself, even if her stomach was rumbling!

'Do you live here alone?' asked Gemma, who was fishing around to get a better picture of his circumstances.

'Yes, of course. I've lived here since 2000 when I came to England from Italy. My parents moved here first to a bungalow around the corner and a few months later, I moved here too. I found it hard at first because I wanted to stay in Italy, so I lived with family friends for a while, but I eventually thought it was a good idea. I was told that things were easier here. Oxford is a university town so there are always things happening. To be honest, where we lived in Tuscany, I found it too rural. I love it here. Anyway, come and sit down in the lounge. It's not good to stand in the hallway. I'll show you where I work, and we will finish your chart. I want to look at your transits for the next six months to get an idea of what is coming up. We can also look at the relationship you mentioned if we have time,' Alessandro explained, confidently.

'That will be brilliant,' replied Gemma, who was amazed that an astrology chart could reveal so much information. She was genuinely interested to hear more. Alessandro pulled up a wooden chair for her, to sit next to him at his desk. He sat on a large black computer chair which he swivelled around to get closer to the computer screen.

'Ah yes, Mars in Taurus, I remember now and look at that, you also have a grand water trine which is interesting.' continued Alessandro.

Gemma moved her head a little closer to Alessandro's so that she could see. To her, it just looked like a load of lines, triangles, and symbols, but she could see what he meant by the water trine. She was interested in Astrology and had grasped the basics.

'You have a lot of aspects to Chiron,' he said.

'Chiron, who's he?'

'Chiron is the wounded healer. To have this number of aspects is extremely rare. Your path is about healing and humanity as a whole' he said, while looking profoundly serious.

'But a wounded one?' she asked, trying to make light of it, but Alessandro continued to look deadly serious. Gemma was surprised by his attitude. He obviously took his astrology more seriously than she imagined. There were piles of charts all over the floor which had dates on top of them. He was busy. He noticed her staring at his paperwork and said, 'excuse the mess Gemma, but I'm in the middle of so many charts right now, and the pile of over there, need to be sent to different countries. I go away to Italy for a couple of weeks, and I come back to dozens of requests. All my clients want them urgently. Then there are the people who phone me about tarot readings. I'm rushed off my feet!'

Alessandro began to look very flustered, and Gemma decided to move back from the screen, sensing his irritation. She didn't want to add to his workload by expecting him to cook her lunch. But Alessandro seemed keen to make a barbeque and was insistent it wasn't any trouble. He told her that it would take no time at all, and she shouldn't worry so much. He declared that the charcoal burned very quickly, much faster than coals. Gemma stood up and walked towards the door, and she suddenly felt a sturdy pair of arms fasten around her waist which pulled her back. She swung around and was surprised that Alessandro leaned towards her and kissed her passionately!

'Ah, I love brunettes. You are so perfect. I cannot believe your astrology chart, it's so much like mine. Our north nodes are only two degrees apart. That means we are both moving in the same direction. Whatever I experience, you will also experience, but you are a sensitive crab, and I'm a fierce lion!' said Alessandro jokingly. Then he grinned at her with his beautiful white teeth!

Gemma looked closely at Alessandro. There was something very lion-like about this man. He loved attention, and he wanted to be king! He had both charm and sexuality, so she knew that he would never be short of admirers. She pulled away from him, and he laughed. 'You're getting all hot and flustered, aren't you? Let's get this barbeque going, or we'll never have time to eat if you are leaving at four?' he said decisively.

The fire soon became hot, and the charcoal was burning quickly! Gemma sat on a cushioned patio chair in a beautiful garden which carried the scent of roses and honeysuckle. Alessandro didn't appear to have time for gardening, so Gemma wondered how he kept it so appealing. There was a vast expanse of green lawn, fruit trees, and a huge patio area. There was also a pond with koi carp which looked well-tended.

Gemma had now moved to a picnic bench in the sun, and watched Alessandro add more charcoal because it was burning so quickly. She had to admit that although she had doubts about their meeting, everything was going well. Gemma knew how to make a fire because she made one every morning, but she wasn't going to interfere. It was wiser not to suggest helping him out because Leo the Lion undoubtedly knew best.

'Gemma, can you please fetch the meat from the kitchen. You'll find it on the bottom shelf of the fridge,' said Alessandro. Gemma hastily walked into the kitchen to look for the meat. As she passed the kitchen table, she couldn't help but notice there was a lightly folded letter resting on the top. It looked as if Alessandro had been reading it recently because his glasses were resting on the top. At least that is what her intuition told her. It was likely a request for a chart. She wanted to read it, she had no idea why, because it was wrong, but she couldn't help herself. He could have a girlfriend in Italy so she didn't want to get involved with him straight after John unless he was free! If he was already in a relationship, then she'd enjoy today, but try not to form an attachment. Although Gemma knew that this might prove difficult, as he was extremely attractive and she already felt a pull towards him. As Alessandro was waiting, she grabbed the meat, then rushed out into the garden, and wondered if after a little wine, he would tell her a more about his life.

Gemma drank a little wine and began to relax. As she was driving half a glass was more than enough! The barbeque chicken in the homemade sauce was fantastic! Alessandro knew how to cook, and he obviously enjoyed great food.

As the sun shone down on them, he began to tell Gemma a little about his family life in Italy. He said that when he came to England in 2000, he had a complete career change. He didn't want to be in a job where he felt stuck. He regularly travelled to Italy to give astrology readings because his family and friends wanted business advice and they knew that 'he had the gift!' He was officially living in England, but he often stayed with friends near Tuscany, where his family had run the Vineyard. There was so much competition in that region that his parents eventually decided to sell up and come to England. They'd bought a bungalow about fifteen minutes from him. He told Gemma they were happy because they got a reasonable price for the business, and they liked England. They occasionally missed Italy but realised the vineyard was too much for them and they were retired. Alessandro explained that he still did a small amount of wine trading for friends and small businesses, and he was interested in getting investors.

Gemma looked at her watch. It was already three forty-five, and they were still munching their way through the food. She decided she had no choice but to appear a little rude and leap off as soon as they had finished eating. She left her plate on the picnic table and told Alessandro she was off to the bathroom. He'd just helped himself to another plate of chicken and salad and was so busy tucking in that he hardly looked up! Gemma told him that she would be back shortly, and he just nodded. She had to walk through the kitchen to reach the downstairs toilet, and as she did so, she once again noticed the letter and glasses. Gemma washed her hands quickly, then very slowly and cautiously removed the glasses and unfolded the letter, which was still resting on top of the kitchen table. She knew Alessandro would still be eating, but even so, she had to be quick. Fortunately, the letter was in English.

Dear Alessandro

I have phoned you loads of times, but you never answer. Have you changed your number? I've also called at your house, but you are never there, so I have posted this through your letterbox! I can't understand why you don't want to see your daughter. She is now six weeks old and gorgeous; you'd love her!

I know you are ignoring me, but I thought you would at least see Charlotte. You're acting as if it was my fault when you know it wasn't. My Mum says you should take responsibility for what happened. I understand you were shocked but so was I!

My Dad said if you don't agree to pay some money towards your daughter, he'll come over to talk to you. He said I should see a Solicitor and he's made an appointment for me. I told him that I don't want any hassle, but if you keep ignoring me, what can I do? He said you are Charlotte's father so you should pay something towards her even if you don't want to see me. Aylesbury Summer Fair is on soon. The place where we met. I expect that I'll run into you there!

Please answer this letter because I'd like us to be friends if nothing else.

Susie

Gemma quickly folded the letter and placed it on the table. She was worried that Alessandro might wonder why she had been gone for a long time. It was shocking that he was the father of a child, and worst still, that he didn't want to see her! This girl Susie had only just left University; so how old would that make her, twenty-one? Gemma suddenly felt sick to the stomach. She realised that she didn't know much about this man at all! He looked noticeably young for his age, but it was shocking to discover that he was ignoring a woman who was the mother of his child.

Gemma walked out into the garden and noticed Alessandro was now reading the property page of a

Spanish newspaper. As she approached him, he folded it and put it on one side. He still had a big pile of food in front of him and was eating very slowly. Gemma decided she had to get back to the girls and it was time to leave.

'Alessandro, I must collect my children now. I hate being late. Sorry to rush off while you are still eating,' she said apologetically.

'Going so soon?' he replied through mouthfuls of food. He then stood up to hug her as he breathed garlic in her face!

'It's a shame because I had plans for us later. Sex is so much better after a healthy meal, don't you think?' He then put his arms around her again and slid them down, squeezing her buttocks hard and lifting her slightly towards him. Gemma could feel his toned body, and in the heat, sweat began to break out on her forehead, which dripped down the edges of her hair. There was no doubt that she had a physical attraction for this man, but she was still disgusted at him! How could this be. It was something she'd never experienced before and there was something unhealthy about it, but she couldn't deny the excitement which ran through her body when he was close, and it unnerved her.

'Another time,' she said, not wishing to say either yes, or no. She knew that she needed to get away from him as quickly as possible. He made her feel giddy and all over the place. His energy drew her so intensely she was unsure if she could keep away, which could very soon become a new dilemma!

BREAKING FREE

Gemma trotted around the ring to warm up Whisper. The instructor told her that he'd been a little lazy lately, but Gemma thought the poor horse was no doubt bored of trotting around the ring every day! Lynne explained it would be good for Whisper to go out for a hack and they would both find it fun.

A small group of them planned to leave the riding school and ride along a bridleway, after which, they would then canter across the fields. Gemma was excited about this and had wanted to join them. She had only been cantering for a brief period but was eager to continue. She noticed the other riders down by the gate and made her way over to them. Whisper was keen to leave the riding school. Fortunately, Lynne decided to come with them on her horse so she could keep an eye on them. Although Gemma trusted Whisper, Lynne told her that when horses were in a group, they had a will of their own and they sometimes galloped. Gemma was a little worried that Whisper could run out of control. It scared her, but Lynne assured her that they'd both be fine.

It was a beautiful sunny morning as the group of horses walked out of the riding school in the direction of the bridleway, which led out to some nearby fields. As soon as Whisper saw the other horses trotting, he wanted to go at quite a pace. Gemma was surprised how easily the horses cantered outside of the riding school in comparison to the ring. It felt more natural, and it was more relaxed. She was happy for Whisper, who was enjoying his freedom. Riding gave her such a buzz. It was a feeling she seldom experienced, which gave her a different focus from the children and her work at the cafe. She liked her job but found it annoying to be doing the same tasks every day. She enjoyed meeting diverse types of people, but the clearing up was dull. She didn't know how long she would stay there but for now, if fitted the bill. She planned to start courses at the College during the winter months, which she hoped would lead her to a better-paid job. There could be something secretarial, or she could return to banking. Gemma was good at figure work, and she really enjoyed the challenge of learning something new. Returning to banking would give her a better income and more stability.

Riding for Gemma kept her sane because it kept her grounded and took her mind off men, particularly her day in Oxford with Alessandro! She had tried to rid him from her thoughts, but she still felt a strong attraction towards him, and it was proving to be impossible. She knew her friends would describe him has a flirt, but there was also something mysterious about him, especially his exceptional knowledge of esoteric subjects. It was also interesting that he'd learnt the tarot at such an early age which was unusual. Alessandro had explained to Gemma his cards had belonged to his mother and they'd been passed down to him through his family. As a child he'd sat for hours gazing at the incredible pictures until he remembered every detail. Alessandro considered the images an essential part of the reading. He said that the astrology came later when he was a little older. Gemma thought it was strange that he hadn't mentioned Susie, the day they had lunch because she'd noticed he was agitated about something, which he said was due to the number of charts he had to finish. Was it the letter from Susie that had irritated him, rather than his work? Gemma still found it hard to get her head around it. Part of her knew it would be sensible to give this man a wide berth, but she was drawn to him in a way that had never happened before! She sometimes had to pinch herself to see if she was the same person who had been married to Tony, because she'd changed so much over the last few months. Her life with him had been dull but there weren't so many dilemmas. Now she had to make all the decisions on her own, and she constantly worried about getting things right, not only for herself, but for the girls.

Why had she attracted men who were so irresponsible and had no intention of having a relationship. This was difficult to understand. Was she rigid or old fashioned? Should she lower her expectations as her meditation teacher had suggested, or did she need to learn to go with the flow. But if she went with the flow with these men, she'd quickly end up in a tricky situation. They would use her, and no doubt she'd be left with a broken heart.

Gemma thought about John's children. She really missed them and wondered if they noticed that she'd disappeared from their father's life. While Gemma was working in the café, or at horse riding, there wasn't time to procrastinate, but when she was at home on her own it was a different story and she was sometimes bombarded by negative thoughts.

The previous night, her children had gone to see their father, and she'd taken out her tarot cards. Gemma was now using the set of cards along with the books which were given to her by Tony's mother! She thought it sad that Jane said they were unlucky, and Gemma hoped they would bring her luck!

Gemma laid out the cards using the Celtic cross spread. She found it hard to believe that her immediate future was still showing her as in the Hermit! When was it possible to get out of this tunnel, and make sense of things? The book explained that the Hermit was also a place of contemplation and learning where she could meditate and find her true self, but this was challenging. It felt like an exceptionally long phase in her life and she wanted to be released from it.

When Gemma first left Tony, she imagined there would be more opportunities to socialise, but this proved impossible, because she didn't have any spare money to spend on going out! With the food bills plus riding and running a car, she had to be careful. Spending money on fuel to see Alessandro wasn't a clever idea when other things should take priority. She knew she had to live within her budget, or she would be unable to pay her bills the following month. She decided it might be an idea to give readings to a few people she knew. It would be extra income, and it would also improve her social life.

The telephone rang unexpectedly, and Gemma was surprised to find it was John.

'Where have you been?' he asked in a worried tone. 'I haven't seen you for months. I'm sorry if I have been a bit distant and wrapped up in my work, but I miss our chats. I'm about tonight if you'd like to come over. I'll open a bottle of red, and you can stay over if you want,' John continued in a friendly tone.

Gemma didn't know what to say. She wasn't sure if it was a clever idea to stay over when she was still trying to get over him. Her heart said yes, at the same time, her head said no! He had a spare evening away from his colleague, and needed her company?

Gemma thought once again about being second best. Was she always going to be second best, the consolation prize? John told her his children were going to be there tonight, and Gemma wanted to see them! She needed to go even if it was to prove to herself, she was over him, which left her with two hours to scrub up and put on some decent clothes. She wasn't sure if he was going to cook, so she decided to grab a sandwich before she left. As she arrived at John's house, she soon realised that none of her feelings for him had disappeared and the old anticipation came flooding back. It had been at least six weeks since she last saw him, and he had grown whiskers!

'Do you like the new look?' he said, then smiled in his captivating way.

Gemma smiled back at him. She was unsure, she wasn't fond of beards. However, she knew that stubble was trendy. Why couldn't John say if he was still seeing Sandra, instead of discussing his change of facial hair. She decided to wait and drop it into the conversation later, so she didn't appear desperate.

'Well, what have you been up to,' John asked her. He appeared a little curious about her absence!

'I've been riding more than usual, and I've also been to a Mind Body and Soul event. Oh yes, and I now have a job in a cafe in Witney, down at the waterfront. We are completely flat out,' she replied.

'I bet you are. It's a real tourist trap right there by the river,' John replied. He sounded a little surprised at her working.

'It's over you know. The thing with Sandra. She was using me. I found out that she was already in a long-term relationship, and I was her bit on the side.' he declared with a tinge of sadness.

Gemma tried to hide her feeling of relief and wondered if she should tell him about her lunch with Alessandro, but then decided not to because it wasn't as if they were in a relationship, and she didn't owe him anything! She hadn't seen any more of him, and if she had, John would no doubt be pleased for her. She suddenly felt as if the shoe was on the other foot, and she found it easier to talk about her life. Being simply good friends meant she was a free agent.

They sat together, played music, and chatted all evening and eventually watched a film which was one of Gemma's favourites. She was careful not to drink because she intended going home. She didn't want to be used by John because he was vulnerable right now. She got the impression that if she stayed, they would sleep in the same bed, but what then? Although she still had feelings for him, she was no longer that silly little girl stuck in a game. She got up and walked towards the door and said goodbye.

'Are you sure you don't want to stay the night?' asked John looking deeply into her eyes. Gemma found it extremely difficult to leave but took a long deep breath as she went to open the front door. There was no doubt that he needed comforting, but she didn't have it in her. She also needed love, and who was giving that to her? Everything was always about what he wanted. She was unlikely to forget about the perfect figure of a woman who was so brilliant, that he was dumb struck by her. It was now her turn, to be that woman and to find the courage to say no and walk away! If he wanted her now, he'd have to chase her because she wasn't anyone's consolation prize. For the first time since she met him, Gemma began to feel powerful and in control and not second best!

Gemma jumped in the Fiesta and drove home. It was midnight on a Saturday night, and the sky was clear of clouds, so she could see the stars. Lacey and Lily were at their father's this weekend, which was a relief. She felt tired, as if everything had caught up with her. Gemma climbed the stairs, which brought her out into her landing bedroom. She'd paid a builder to make a new wall with a doorway, so she could have privacy, or she would hear the girls each time they went up to their room.

The room was a beautiful sunshine yellow, and she'd added a border by using some stencils to make it attractive. It was a lovely airy room with a corner window which overlooked the fields on one side and the wood on the other. The cottage felt cold at this time of night because the heating had gone off, but she snuggled under the duvet, which usually did the trick. Besides, it was spring now, and although the odd night was cold, most of the time it was warm. Despite the cold, Gemma knew she'd sleep well, because she had held on to her power and not given in to John. Afterall, he'd been the one who said that he only wanted friendship then things changed, and he expected her to come running. It was confusing. Well, she was worth more than that. She wanted to be with someone who valued and understood her. If not, she'd stay single. She had a job and a great hobby, but more importantly, she had two beautiful daughters. What more could a woman want?

ALESSANDRO

Alessandro looked at the charts piled on his study floor and wondered where to start. He was usually enthusiastic about his work because he received good money for each chart, and there were frequent follow-ups. Sometimes one for a spouse, or one of the children had a chart for a birthday gift. He also created compatibility charts for partners which were popular. He loved looking at the dynamics between the charts. It would sometimes appear two people fitted like a glove, but then there was a difficult aspect, which could create a significant challenge. As a result of what he'd learned over the years, he tried not to take his personal relationships too seriously because connections were complex and some could even be past life.

Alessandro had been hurt very badly in the past. He was convinced that he would marry Maria. The relationship was exactly what he wanted, mutual attraction, trust, and sexual chemistry, or so he thought. Unfortunately, there had been a miscalculation, despite him carefully studying Maria's birth chart, Alessandro had no idea that she had a strong attraction to women. At first, he thought it would be entertaining to share her, but several months later when the reality kicked in, he found it insulting. Maria would never seriously commit, let alone consider such an old-fashioned idea as marriage. He'd often tried to get hold of her on the telephone, but she seldom acknowledged his calls. The trust they had at the beginning of their relationship quickly diminished and he had to admit defeat. Maria was bi-sexual, and he absolutely hated it. His male pride wouldn't allow him to accept it. It would have been easier if she had cheated on him because he could have at least been angry, but this situation lingered on in his mind. Had Maria loved him? Did she know what she was doing? She had told him that she loved him, but he didn't want to be her brother. One thing that he'd learned from this experience, was that there were so many types of love. Women were such complex creatures. He felt like a failure at relationships, and he didn't see himself becoming involved with anyone soon. Now, he had this young girl hounding him for money when she had just been a bit of fun.

Alessandro remembered the day he first met Susie at the Aylesbury Summer Fair, a small art and music festival near Oxford. He was working outside, giving readings, sitting at his table in the sun, and a beautiful young woman with long red hair, came over to talk to him. Her face resembled a woman from a 'Botticelli' painting and she wore a short woolly low-cut top showing her mid-drift, with a pale blue pair of jeans, and a studded belt. An exotic display of crystal necklaces hung from her neck, but the one that caught his eye was the beautiful green amber, which rested on her skin just above her breasts. As she talked to him, the necklaces swayed attractively, and he felt almost hypnotised. Susie's sunglasses sat neatly on top of her head. She was not what the English called 'a hippy' in the true sense of the word. She had class, and he later discovered she came from a typical middle-class family!

They chatted endlessly, while standing in the sun. There was much to talk about because Susie knew so much about astrology. Her mother wrote astrology columns for national magazines. In the end, Alessandro couldn't help but ask her for a date which was something he hadn't entertained since he had dated Maria. Women were escorts, you didn't take them out, but Susie had stirred something that he'd forgotten, and he was enthralled.

As a result of their meeting, they had a short enthusiastic affair. Susie had not long left University and was looking for work using her Degree in Psychology. As time went on, Alessandro found her intense, and he avoided long conversations with her. He adored her face and body, but he didn't want her analysing his deeper levels because it scared him. Susie knew Alessandro was running away from something because he rarely talked about his family or past relationships. Their meetups were about one thing only, and that was sex. He knew he needed to move on before she became too serious, but he didn't want to hurt her. Susie was already beginning to show signs of forming a close attachment. Although she often repeated 'I don't need you to commit to me,' he knew she had strong feelings towards him.

Alessandro felt it was unhealthy for a young girl to feel like that over an older man, and he didn't need that!

They made love in the afternoons after Susie had finished her University Lectures. She was adept at giving him pleasure, and there were no positions or techniques left unexplored. Their connection made Alessandro feel years younger, and he would have continued with her as a lover if she hadn't asked so many questions. She wanted to go on his trips with him, which was never going to happen. His trips were a side of his life that he kept private. It wasn't a problem talking about astrology, but that was about it. He decided to tell Susie he planned to return to Italy. He knew that she'd never want to follow him because the girl was undecided about her future, and she was going to enrol for a Masters if she couldn't find a job.

The baby came as a massive shock, and he didn't want to talk to discuss it! When he briefly spoke to Susie on the phone, he asked 'What's changed? Their get-togethers had always been about sex and she knew that!' They had never been in a relationship, nor would they be, because he was happy on his own. He had promised her nothing. He understood why she'd want some money for the baby because she was a student and didn't have a job. He already decided that he'd give her something because if not, things could turn very unpleasant, and someone could come after him. Why did women try to pull him into situations that he clearly didn't want, besides, the girl should have told him she wasn't taking the pill. It was natural to assume she was.

Weren't all young women of that age! She hadn't said anything about it at the time. Why not?

Susie was one of the best lovers that Alessandro had met. She pleased him in so many ways, without having to ask which was unusual for someone so young! When he thought about it now, the whole situation annoyed him. He sighed profusely then got out his cheque book. He'd send her two hundred pounds to start with and tell her he'd be in touch soon. At least it would stop her father visiting him. He couldn't face getting into a tricky situation with an older man, especially an English one. When he thought about her now, it made him angry. All the attraction had gone, and he wasn't interested in anything else.

Alessandro continued putting the charts on the floor in date order. He'd take a few to the post when he sent the cheque. He came upon Gemma's chart, which he thought was extremely interesting. The girl had talents, so it was odd that she worked in a cafe. Shame she was a mother because without children, they'd have so much in common. He couldn't go there with all that responsibility. At this stage in his career, he could ill afford to be hurt again, especially when his chart indicated world travel and soon. Alessandro was confident about where he was going, and compromising wasn't part of his plan.

DINNER WITH FRIENDS

Gemma was amazed to receive an unexpected email from Alessandro asking her to dinner. He explained he was having a group of people over for a dinner party, and she was welcome to stay the night because his friends were also staying and it was safer not to drive. It made sense because of the distance, and if she wanted to drink, could she please bring a bottle of wine.

The following Friday evening, Gemma found herself once again driving to Alessandro's house. Part of her knew she was being reckless, but surely it was better than spending the whole weekend on her own. It also kept her away from John. She was surprised how quick the journey was, and she briskly walked up to Alessandro's door to press the bell.

'Come in Gemma, I'm in the middle of cooking right now, but my friends will be here soon, so why don't you sit down and have a glass of wine. 'You'll love Antonio and Rosie. They're great fun. You'll have to stay in the spare room tonight. You can't drive home late, and we will be late,' Alessandro said as he gave her a gentle smack on the backside. This alarmed her. She didn't know what to say. She'd decided to keep Alessandro as a spiritual friend and resist his advances. She didn't know him and he'd already started playing with her. The discovery of the letter had thrown a different light on things. Gemma didn't want to get into another game! She was pleased that his friends were coming tonight, because they wouldn't be alone, which made her feel more relaxed. If anything were to happen between them, it certainly wouldn't be when his friends were about. Gemma believed they would have to get to know each other slowly if anything was going to develop.

When Antonio and his English wife Rosie arrived around seven p.m., Gemma was already very hungry because she was used to eating early, and she wondered how long it would be before the food was ready!

Sometime later, the four of them sat around a polished wooden table in the dining room. Alessandro had tastefully set the table using fresh flowers in small glass vases. There were also napkins and some beautiful silver candle holders. Gemma noticed a fantastic smell drifting through from the kitchen, which she hoped was their dinner! After ten minutes, Alessandro served Tuscan grilled trout with sauce, a unique recipe which he explained had been handed down from his grandmother. The fish extremely impressed Gemma. Alessandro certainly knew how to cook. As she took another mouthful, she heard Antonio tease him.
'What secret family recipe?' he asked.

Alessandro smiled, then gave him a wink! They obviously knew each other well, she thought, feeling slightly uncomfortable by their familiarity. She later discovered Antonio had worked at his parents' vineyard in Tuscany. He'd met Rosie whilst working there because she was on holiday in the region and had visited the vineyard. As Rosie was from the United Kingdom, he happily relocated. The couple had so many things in common. A love of sailing, cooking and animals and it wasn't long before they started living together. Since moving to Oxford, they had set up an animal rescue sanctuary. The centre was made famous after being featured on a television program last year. Gemma listened to their story and assumed that both Rosie and Antonio had veterinary qualifications. The sanctuary rehabilitated dogs and horses. Gemma thought this was fantastic and was keen to learn more. It was great that the couple had the energy to follow their dreams and she began to relax in their presence.

While Antonio and Rosie were chatting, Gemma and Alessandro's eyes met several times across the table. Every time she looked at him, she noticed he was already looking at her. He'd also been regularly filling her wine glass, and they were now nearing the end of their third bottle. Antonio and Rosie shared some very elaborate stories about their encounters with animals. Gemma told them how much she enjoyed her riding lessons at home in Witney, while Alessandro openly surveyed her body and made her feel uncomfortable.

Gemma wore a beautiful black sparkly dress which she'd bought a few years ago when she was living with Tony. It must have been for a work's Christmas party or something, she couldn't remember. It hugged her figure nicely and made her legs appear long and shapely. Alessandro suddenly dropped his napkin under the table. As he picked it up, his hand stroked the lower part of Gemma's leg. She felt flustered by his actions because he caught her off guard and was slightly embarrassed. Alessandro glanced over at her, and she noticed his perfect smile. He was immaculately dressed this evening, wearing white jeans with a smart long sleeved navy shirt and good quality Italian shoes. He'd also gelled his hair.

Gemma quickly turned her head to avoid his suggestive glances but it was difficult to avoid him without appearing rude.

After the most incredible gelato ice cream, the group finally left the table! It had a different consistency to the other ice creams Gemma had tasted. Had she died and gone to heaven! One thing was for sure; she hadn't had a meal like that since living on her own. It was a real treat to have someone cook for her. Although she enjoyed cooking, she had so little time to experiment and she was stuck in a routine of preparing the same meals each week which bored her, and the girls!

They left the dining table for the comfort of the living room and sat on two adjacent sofas, where the conversation turned to Antonio and Rosie's relationship.

'I'm so fortunate to have met you Rosie,' started Antonio.

'But where would I be without you, Antonio? We are two of a kind, and if I hadn't been on holiday, we might never have met. Now we're living together. Isn't it strange how things work out. We're so busy with the animals, there's little time to relax. Well, only when we visit Alessandro,' said Rosie, knocking back the end of her glass.

Gemma noticed that Rosie had marks on her lower arms and wondered whether they were insect bites. That's awful, she thought. Had Rosie been bitten whilst working outside. There were also several long scratches. Gemma's gaze had unsettled her because she suddenly pulled down her sleeves, then smiled, as if she'd felt a chill.

'What, an occasional glass of wine, that's a joke! I'm still waiting for you two to turn up with a few bottles of your own,' Alessandro jested. Gemma felt guilty for staring at Rosie and quickly averted her eyes. 'You're a couple of boozers! You're always drinking my wine. You two drink more of it than I do!' Alessandro continued, then laughed!

Gemma felt awkward. The three of them were obviously familiar with each other, which was great, but their banter made her feel left out. She wondered how Lacey and Lily were getting on at their father's. She couldn't stop thinking about her children. Tony had promised to take them swimming. They loved that, so they were having fun and she decided to stop worrying. She turned her attention back to the group and then offered to take the plates through to the kitchen to start the washing up. Alessandro followed her closely behind while carrying the remaining dishes. They left Antonio and Rosie talking. Alessandro shouted to them that he'd put the kettle on for coffee. As Gemma put the dishes in the sink and started to run the taps, she suddenly felt Alessandro close behind her, lifting her dress! She was horrified and embarrassed by his behaviour and hastily pulled it down, but his hands continued to roam all over her body, sliding up and down her thighs in a rhythmical motion. He was also making noises in her ear.

'Ah, you gorgeous brunette. I love you English women. You are sexier than the Italians. Look at me. I'm aroused, he said, undoing his zip!

Gemma quickly pulled away and adjusted her dress. She didn't know where to look, and the colour was rising in her face. Alessandro grinned at her in amusement. Damn you, she thought. Please leave me alone. She was regretting coming out this evening and dreaded the thought of staying the night! Was she safe? She thought Antonio and Rosie were also staying but it suddenly dawned on her that she might be left on her own with Alessandro! It was clear that they'd all had a fair amount to drink. Was this the Italian way? It hadn't affected them much, but she felt light-headed, and was struggling to keep control. Gemma tried to compose herself as she walked back into the lounge with Alessandro following her close behind.

Over the past few months, Gemma had become acutely aware of her senses but was she missing something? Had Alessandro been the man in her reading? If it was him, then he already knew she was coming today and the probable outcome! Gemma suddenly felt set up by a set of circumstances she didn't fully understand. Was karma forcing her hand? Did she have to carry on with the connection whatever the outcome to achieve balance? Had she asked for this! She thought once again about her old meditation teacher's words, 'be careful what you wish for, because it might come true.' Gemma knew that she secretly craved excitement. However, the practical side of her was still saying steady and secure. It was confusing because part of her wanted to run, and another part of her wanted to see this through!

Antonio and Rosie continued to drink their coffee, then they suddenly stood up to say goodbye. Gemma was surprised they were leaving. They said they had enjoyed their evening but had called a taxi because Rosie insisted that Antonio was too drunk to walk, even though they lived only a few roads away.

'Well, said Alessandro, I hope you enjoyed your meal, Gemma. Antonio and Rosie are such good friends of mine, and we always have fun together. Sometimes we play games, but tonight was more about talking. You must be tired now, I am. I'll show you to your room. It's next to mine, but don't worry. I'll sleep in my own room tonight.'

Alessandro led Gemma up the stairs to a little room with a small single bed. She saw a small bedside table and a lamp, and it appeared plain but comfortable. Gemma walked over to the bed and placed her things on the floor. As she leaned over, she suddenly felt Alessandro grab her violently from behind. She thought he'd already gone to his own room, and she was shocked. His whole demeanour had changed. He was no longer playful as he'd been in the kitchen. This was different, and Gemma was scared. Before she had time to think, Alessandro forced her to the bed with his whole-body weight. She couldn't breathe with his weight resting on her, and she turned her head to the side, gasping for air. Alessandro grabbed the back of her hair with one hand, and forcibly lifted her head. He then rested on one side of her body and used his free arm for ripping off her underwear. He then forced himself into her. Gemma cried 'no, stop it, you're hurting me, but he had his full weight on her, and he continued to pull her hair violently. Gemma's neck hurt. She felt as if she was being smothered, and it was clear that Alessandro wasn't going to stop.

'I know you want me, Gemma. You were looking at me all night. Don't make such a fuss. Be quiet, or the neighbours will hear you. I know you're having fun,' he whispered sarcastically,' he continued to talk to her like a child.

Gemma wasn't having fun. Her head hurt, and the weight of Alessandro on top of her was unbearable. It felt as though he was squeezing the life out of her as he forced himself into her repeatedly. He finally groaned, stopped, then rolled off the bed.

'Thanks,' he said, as he slowly walked away, leaving the door slightly ajar. He didn't say anything more to Gemma as he left the room.

Gemma's heart was pounding. She noticed the room was extremely dark, and she slowly reached one arm upwards to turn on the lamp. She was surprised she wasn't bleeding, but she felt battered. What made him think he could treat her this way? The man was an animal. Had he planned this, or was he drunk? Gemma trembled with fear and felt sick. She wanted to go to the bathroom, but she was afraid to step out of the room fearing Alessandro might hear her and come back to her room. She decided that her safest bet was to stay in the bedroom until the morning. Hopefully, she'd get a little sleep, and the morning would come quickly. As soon as it was light, she'd drive home as fast as she could. All she wanted was to be at home in her own bed, in her little cottage where she felt safe.

Why had she come here? If only she'd listened to herself. She suddenly felt humiliated and desperately upset.

Gemma was awoken in the early hours of the morning by a beam of light shining through the curtains. She couldn't see the place where the light came in, but it made a huge round circle on the wall of the little bedroom. She drew back the curtain to see what was happening, and noticed that the sun hadn't risen yet, so the ball of light was odd! Gemma looked at the clock on the bedside table and started to recall the events of the previous night, which felt like an hour ago!

It was four thirty a.m., and she could hear loud snoring, despite having closed her bedroom door. Gemma very quietly got up and made her way to the bathroom. With a bit of luck, if she crept out quietly without her shoes, Alessandro wouldn't hear her.

Gemma left the bathroom silently and tiptoed down the stairs being careful where she stepped. She was relieved to reach the hallway without making a sound, then she quickly lifted the latch and was out in the early morning air. As she breathed in, she felt a massive sense of relief. Her Fiesta was sitting in the driveway where she left it. She felt cold, ached, and was dying for a cup of tea but thought it was better to get on the road because the roadside cafes opened at five a.m.

Gemma jumped in her car, reversed then put her foot down. She wanted to get away from Alessandro's house as fast as possible. Her heart continued to beat loudly but thankfully all was quiet, and she hadn't disturbed him, because the house was still in darkness.

As soon as Gemma was a few miles down the road, she felt better. When she arrived home, she planned to bury her head under the duvet until she could face the world. It would be easier for her to pretend none of this nightmare had happened than to admit her stupidity. She knew that Alessandro had raped her, but she vowed that she'd never tell anyone. Being involved in a situation like this was horrific and humiliating. What on earth would people think, and more to the point what if it got back to her children? She had to keep quiet and pretend it hadn't happened, which would mean keeping strong. Once again, Gemma felt she was being challenged beyond all measures. When will this stop?

The fool obviously had negative aspects as well as positive ones! Yes, the cards were unlucky, she whispered as she began to follow the signs home!

BACK WITH THE CHILDREN

Gemma was happy that Lacey was doing so well at school, but sadly Lily was falling behind. After attending a recent parents' evening, she discovered Lily found her classwork a bit of a struggle, particularly Maths, because her other subjects were better. As Gemma was excellent at figures, she found it hard to understand, but decided to help Lily with her schoolwork. They could go through her maths together, so her daughter could get on top of things. They'd start with the basics because if she had a better understanding it would help with her grades. In recent month's she'd been far too pre-occupied with men when she should have been helping the girls. She was still in shock from what happened in Oxford. Alessandro hadn't been in touch. Gemma had no doubt that he'd pushed the incident away and moved on. They were unlikely to meet again, unless she started doing readings at events and ran into him by chance, which was doubtful because she'd thrown her tarot cards in the fire. They felt unlucky and the death card had appeared so many times in her readings, that she was fed up with seeing it. Her only means of escape was to destroy them. It was true, doing readings for yourself, was unlucky! She hated that card, despite knowing that it could mean the end of a situation, rather than death, it still made her uncomfortable. Was it the end of her association with Alessandro, she hoped so!

After Gemma had been to the parents' evening to discuss Lily's progress, she concluded that her life was like a bad episode of a soap opera, and she had to get her act together before she was consumed. People had created webs around her, and they were pulling her in. The only way she could break free was to keep her distance and focus on the essential things like helping the girls. Her children were the most important thing in her life, and she wanted them to know it. She knew that she'd been behaving irresponsibly, and it was time for her to rein herself in! There had been times when she had felt like the couple at the bus stop, continually asking for what was coming up, and her readings had become her reality. Enough was enough, and it was time to take responsibility for her path, rather than to allow herself to be pulled into situations where she lost control.

Her father always said, 'you make your life,' but Gemma was sure life was destined. On the other hand, living a life packed full of predictions and assumptions had led to disastrous consequences. If she'd kept her integrity instead of allowing herself to be bowled over by Alessandro, she'd be happy now. Why had she got involved with him when she was just getting over John! He was just another distraction from taking control of her life!

As the weeks' past, Gemma began to miss her cards, and eventually she bought a set of fairy cards. She loved the pictures because as a small child, she used to read the flower fairy books and the fairies lived on in her imagination. These cards resonated with her because they reminded her of her childhood. She'd discovered a local mind body soul event that was on in a few weeks, and she contacted the organiser to see if she could give Angel and Fairy readings. Gemma was both excited and apprehensive because she'd only practised readings with her friends. She feared she'd never be ready to work in public let alone for money, but she eventually decided that she needed to find out! Margery from the cafe told her about the event which was organized by one of her friends. Margery had already had a reading with Gemma, a few weeks ago and was so impressed that she was more than willing to recommend her.

Gemma was extremely rushed. She had to help the girls with their homework, work at the cafe, along with many jobs that needed doing at home. Things were mounting up, and she wished there was an extra pair of hands to help, especially with the gardening, or someone to give the girls a lift to see their friends! This was one of the joys of living just out of the town. Most of the girl's friends were in the town, so Gemma was always getting her car out to drive short distances. Whatever was going on this week, she wanted to book a riding lesson for this weekend, because they worked like magic! Gemma regretted letting her tuition slip because it would be tough catching up. Lynne had told her that as she got on so well with cantering a few weeks ago, they were going to try a few simple jumps. They would then move on to the cross-country course just to get the feel of it!

Gemma was excited, but it meant buying a decent pair of riding boots and jodhpurs. She could continue to borrow a hat from the school for the time being because they were expensive! Gemma was a little nervous about being rusty and hoped the cantering would quickly come back to her. If she was going to jump, she needed to be good at it.

After the girls were dropped off at school, Gemma drove up to the riding school. She decided to leave the housework until she got back because there was no time and riding was more important! It made a change going in the wee, rather than the weekend, and Gemma felt excited.

Whisper was happy to see her. She stroked his mane and spoke quietly in his ear.

'Hey Whisper, I want you to be good today because I've been feeling a bit fragile, so take it easy with me,' she whispered quietly.

The sun was out, and it was a glorious morning. It had previously been raining quite heavily, but as Gemma arrived at the riding school, she was surprised how quickly the weather had changed, and Gemma felt blessed!

Gemma quickly mounted Whisper and found she no longer needed the riding block, which was great. She was quite fit now, and she quickly pulled herself up. Whisper made some loud snorting noises through his nose as if he was letting off a bit of steam. He's been cooped up in the ring again, bored, thought Gemma. Whisper followed Lynne up to the other ring which was covered with sand. There were several jumps which were well spaced. It didn't look that difficult, and Gemma felt relieved.

'Right, you need to get up a good speed if you are going to jump and then you must remember to lean forward just before you go over. If you lean back, you'll lose your balance, and you could fall off. I'll demonstrate the jumps on Blackberry first. We'll go over that straightforward jump over there, and then you can follow me. Gemma watched closely. It looked as if she had to lean right forward, but it also didn't look as high as she imagined.

'Come on, give it a go,' shouted Lynne.

Gemma kicked Whisper, who didn't want to move. She then gave him another little kick. Gemma hated kicking horses because it felt cruel, but Lynne assured her it was better to do this than using the riding crop. She gave Whisper the third kick and his ears pricked up, and he quickly moved from trot to canter. When he saw the jump, he went for it, which surprised her. Whisper appeared to enjoy jumping.

'He loves it,' said Gemma.

'I know, he does. All horses love jumping. This time, make sure that you grip more with your legs.'

Gemma did as Lynne suggested and felt happy. Surprisingly, she loved it too. It was far more fun than she thought and not that scary. Whisper had woken up, and he started to shake his head a little as if he wanted to keep going.

'Is Whisper all right? It's just that he seems a bit lively for some reason, like he is getting a little too excited,' she asked.

'Don't worry about that, he knows what he's doing,' said Lynne reassuringly.

Gemma prepared to go over the jump for the third time, and as Whisper leapt, she felt herself come down quite hard in the saddle and started to lose her balance. Instead of Whisper stopping as he had the last time, he suddenly broke into a canter and started gaining speed. Gemma tried not to panic and lent forward slightly gripping the horse and shortening the reins to pull him back, but Whisper wasn't listening. He suddenly turned very sharply to jump a totally different jump, and Gemma came hurtling off. She wasn't sure exactly how she fell off, but her feet were no longer in the stirrups.

Gemma lay on the ground, which was extremely hard. She knew she'd hit her head on the edge of a jump, and for a few minutes she felt sick. Then everything blurred, and she lost consciousness.

When Gemma came around, she found herself covered with a blanket with Lynne on the ground next to her, but there was no sign of Whisper.

'Don't worry, you're all right Gem, but don't move until the ambulance crew have looked at you. I've called them, and they're on their way.

Gemma groaned. She was hurting badly from head to foot, particularly on one side of her head, but her leg also felt twisted. She felt like crying but didn't have enough strength. When two ambulance crew arrived with a stretcher and gently lifted her on to it, she felt relieved. They very carefully placed her head in a protective device and told her to keep it on until they had the results of her x-rays.

'My kids, I have to fetch them from school soon,' cried Gemma.

'Don't worry, we can sort that out for you,' replied Lynne reassuringly. I have your mobile and I'm coming with you to the hospital. Gemma felt relieved, but she also felt powerless. She was so weak and tried to lift her arms. Try not to move until they have examined you, said Lynne. I've seen a lot of falls; usually, people are shocked but get up quickly, so you could have broken something. Let's hope not, but you might be concussed. Gemma was in shock and wanted to rest. When they arrived at the hospital, she was quickly wheeled into a room with several medical staff, and a young doctor came over to examine her.

'We need to take some x-rays of your head and back to make sure nothing is broken. That was quite a fall you had young lady. I want to keep an eye on you overnight to make sure that there isn't anything more serious going on, but for now, I'll put you into a side room. We'll move you as soon as someone's available to take you up to x-ray. Gemma found it hard to understand the Doctor because it was difficult to hear anything with the head protector on. She couldn't nod, only blink and smile, and she hoped it would be taken off shortly. It crossed her mind how upset Lacey and Lily would be to see her like this. For a while, she lay there looking up at the ceiling, taking deep breaths because she didn't like this thing on her head. Lynne was still holding her hand, and Gemma vaguely heard her say something about calling Tony.

Gemma felt extraordinarily sleepy and was unsure who Tony was. Her head was muzzy because they had given her pain killers, and the room became distant as she drifted off to sleep. When she awoke, her head protector had been removed. She'd been wheeled into x-ray but didn't remember a thing. Gemma still felt sick, but the doctor said it was shock and was normal.

Gemma lay still for what felt like hours. Then she heard Tony's voice and realised that he and the children must have arrived. Lily rushed towards her and grabbed her hand.

'Be careful please Lily, Mum's had a fall, and the Doctor said we must get the result of the x-rays before she's allowed to move. She needs to keep as still as possible,' she heard him say.

'But I want Mum to come home,' said Lily who appeared horrified to see Gemma lying there unable to move.

'Mum will be home soon,' Tony replied, but I'm looking after you tonight, and we'll come again in the morning. We need to check Mum's doing all right before she comes home. Gemma squeezed the girls' hands at either side of her. By the sound of Lily's voice, she guessed that she'd been crying, but Lacey didn't say a word. Gemma knew that Lacey cared, it was just her way. Lacey leaned close to her with a blank expression on her face. It was an expression which didn't say much, but Gemma knew that look. It meant she was shocked and upset.

Tony sent the girls to go and stand by the door and briefly walked over to Gemma.

'Don't worry Gemma; I can look after the girls for the next few days. I can't believe you would do something as stupid as riding though! Surely you know riding is a dangerous sport, and you're a mother, what were you thinking of? I hope that you'll have a good think about all this when you get better. I can't have the girls for long because I've got deadlines for Court Cases,' Tony said, none too pleasantly.

Gemma felt too weak to say anything. She'd heard it all before, so there was little point in making the effort to talk to him. How could Tony understand her need for riding? She wanted to do something for her, which was partly the reason why their marriage went wrong. Tony thought she ought to be content with being a mother who worked her life around the family. He considered her selfish to have her own needs. They had often argued about her wanting more freedom. If she had stayed living with Tony, nothing would have been resolved. He had too many expectations of her and they weren't even realistic! If Gemma fell short of his ideals, she suffered. He had a way of being extraordinarily moody and childish, which made her life miserable.

Gemma didn't see Tony leave, but she sensed his absence. She was aware of his energy field, which felt like a dark shadow. He was an explosion about to happen! There was so much anger; it made him rigid. She hoped that one day he would meet someone who would help him loosen up because his inflexibility was a disease, which made him unhappy. It also made him out of balance, yet he thought everyone else was! Gemma sighed and then decided to press the buzzer. She was pleased that she meditated. If she was pulled off balance; meditation brought her back to her centre. She was a little hurt that Tony didn't show her any compassion, but at the same time she was used to it. He couldn't think beyond his own needs. It would be hard enough for him to look after the girls for a couple of days when he was working. Where were the nurses? It was a hectic hospital!

Gemma drifted off to sleep again. When she awoke, she was surprised to find that she'd been put on a ward. She had a vague recollection of two nurses moving her, but she was in and out of dream state. Fortunately, it was a small ward, and the other people around her seemed to be sleeping. It was late in the afternoon, and she turned to look at a mysterious light on the wall, which was near the door and wondered if it was the same light as she had seen several times before on her bedroom wall! This time it was moving around a little like a sunbeam. The light made her smile because Gemma knew that she wasn't alone. Whatever this light was, it was protecting her, and she felt reassured. Was it some kind of energy which followed and protected her when she was in trouble. The light always appeared close to her, either on the walls or even doors. It was mysterious and fascinating, but it was also comforting.

A young Doctor suddenly appeared with her x-ray results. He said although she had some bruising, fortunately, nothing was broken, and she was going to be fine. The doctor also said that she had some internal bruising and asked her if she was aware of it. Gemma didn't want to discuss it but she eventually said that she had been stuck in a complicated relationship. The doctor looked concerned and asked if, she was sure. Gemma tried to get him off the subject by saying, it was down to riding, but by the look on his face, she knew that he wasn't convinced. It was such a horrific night, that Gemma decided several weeks ago that she'd put it behind her and move on. The worst thing that could happen to her now was for people to discover the truth. The doctor also told her that she had to stay in the hospital until tomorrow, then she could be collected and taken home. Gemma decided to call Jo, her riding friend, because there was no way she wanted Tony to return to the hospital. His presence made her feel worse, and she was determined to continue with her riding. It was terrible that she fell off, but no real damage was done. Tony wasn't going to control her life, not now, nor in the future!

TONY

Tony cooked for the girls. It didn't bother him because he loved having them, and he didn't want them to be upset by the accident. He knew that Gemma would recover quickly, and he told them that she'd be home soon. He gave them their favourite dinner, which was sausages chips and beans, not healthy, but it was extremely easy to cook. He couldn't spare much time in the kitchen when he had to work later. Tony quickly scraped the plates and then placed them in the sink. He then served up some yoghurt. After they had finished, he decided to crack on with preparing his paperwork for Court. He had so much work on that he had no alternative but to work from home. Having all this work was a nuisance because not only did he want to spend more time with the girls, but he also wanted to begin dating. If he wanted a woman in his life, he'd have to put a little time aside. Gemma had caused him so much pain, not just with the accident, but because she didn't appear to need him. He tried to convince himself that he no longer had feelings for her, but as soon as he got the call from Lynne about the accident, his heart began to pound. Part of him still loved Gemma and always would.

Damn the woman, why did she have to do this? Why wasn't she more careful? Didn't she know how upsetting it was, not only for him, but for the girls to see her like that! Horse riding was dangerous, but there was little point in him trying to convince her otherwise, because she always did what she wanted. Her stubbornness was the reason why they parted. He didn't understand why she wasn't content with her lot because other women were. He had given her so much, and she'd never appreciated it. They had experienced a good standard of living while they were together. She was ungrateful. A lot of women were envious of what they had together. They had lived in a beautiful house with enough money for the family to live on but she was never happy.

Tony was angry. He harboured a deep feeling of rejection; he wondered if he could ever move on. It was madness, and it was frustrating but what could he do about it! He sometimes quizzed the girls about their mother to find out if she was seeing anyone, but they wouldn't give him a clear answer. Lacey usually said, 'I don't know Dad, and I don't care, and Lily just shrugged. It was Tony's male pride that made him curious. He didn't want Gemma to meet a man and be happy. It was wrong that some bloke should step into the father role when it was his family! He found it hard to see himself back with her now, despite his feelings, but he still had to remind himself they were divorced. Time had flown so quickly it didn't seem possible. She left him with no alternative but to get on and meet other women to try and block her out of his mind! Gemma needed to wake up and appreciate what she was missing out on. No doubt she thought things were running smoothly, but the cottage was cold and cramped, she had very few friends, and she often struggled with the girls. How could she cope with everything and earn an income? But he wasn't going to give her any extra money so that she could spend it on herself. She'd left him, and there were consequences, but he knew deep down that he'd never get over it.

Tony was shocked when he received the final divorce papers from his Solicitor, because it felt like he'd wasted a large part of his life. Although they'd only been married for two years, they had been living together for far longer. Why had he got married to this woman. His friends told him not to bother at the time, it would make things more complicated. He should have listened to them. He didn't intend being friendly towards her. As far as he was concerned, Gemma had lost her social position, which she'd only had because she had been married to him! It was her choice to go it alone and give it up, and for what? He breathed in sharply and went to check on the girls. They appeared happy enough watching television. They'd be fine for a couple of hours, and he'd make sure they went to bed by nine.

Tony turned his attention to his work. He had to prepare the paperwork to send to the Barrister for Court. He was relieved to turn it over to him. It was a nightmare. He felt out of his depth with this case. This man Alessandro had so many identities. No-one knew who he was. Amongst other things, Tony had uncovered fake birth certificates, and the man was involved with secret organisations. He was extraordinarily dodgy, and he also enjoyed playing the nice guy! Going after him was extremely difficult. He was unsure who was backing him, but he had someone powerful protecting him, which made things worse. Tony knew that they would have to work fast before Alessandro reinvented himself again! It was almost impossible to find out who his connections were, but there was no doubt they were powerful. Fortunately, he'd managed to get some statements from women who had also suffered in his hands, which helped, but a few of the women had retracted them before he could use them. Were these women afraid of him? Sylvia Jones certainly wasn't but then she wasn't an ordinary sort of woman. For one, she was a Barrister who knew the legal system, and when he tried to scam her, she wasn't going to let it rest. But it was awkward that Sylvia was so well known in the legal community because instead of people aiding her, they were embarrassed and gave little away. How could a woman in her position be taken in by a dodgy wine merchant and so quickly! The case had been passed from pillar to post until Tony begrudgingly accepted it. He knew from the start that it would be turned over to a barrister due to the severity of the allegations. Deception, fraud, misrepresentation, gross misconduct; failure to follow the law and then there were Alessandro's fake identities, the list went on. This was far more than a scam and the hearing date needed bringing forward quickly; otherwise, this man could once again slip away under the guise of a new identity. It was clear from his investigations that he had spent time not only in the United Kingdom but in Italy, Spain, and Germany.

His astrology work was a cover. It had to be because there was something more sinister lurking underneath. If only he could delve deeper, but he was barred at every turn. Whoever these people were who protected him, they had done an excellent job of covering their tracks!

Tony's meeting with Sylvia Jones was tomorrow afternoon. He'd brought it forward as everything needed to speed up. He would have to read through all the paperwork carefully tonight, so he was on the ball. Sylvia always kept him on his toes!

Tony needed to take the girls back to Gemma first thing tomorrow because he had so much to do. He needed to be focused so that he didn't forget anything. If he could find evidence to support Alessandro's abusive behaviour towards women, he could show the Jury what type of man he was. What he needed was one woman to follow through and happily testify in Court, which would enable the Jury to see he was both dishonest and abusive. Without this evidence, he was unable to show him for the devil he was.

Sylvia wanted Alessandro hung drawn and quartered, so Tony had to find everything he could to throw at him. His client was fuming that this wine merchant took her for a fool. She was also embarrassed not only by the situation, but because her career was also on the line and it made her feel humiliated and angry. There was no way this man was going to get away with this. Sylvia wanted blood!

RECOVERING

Gemma had been discharged from the hospital and was told to take it easy! As soon as she returned home, she cuddled the girls. She didn't want to let them go. They were everything to her, and although her absence had been short, it brought home to her how important they were. Gemma had received so many 'get well cards' which were now lined up along the mantelpiece. There was even one from John, which surprised her, and she wondered how he knew about her riding accident, but she guessed that when you live near a small-town news can travel fast.

Gemma had been off work for several weeks with shock and bad bruising. The whole experience had set her back emotionally, and her doctor told her that she was suffering from post-traumatic stress and needed to take it easy for a while until she was better.

When Lily and Lacey went to school the next day, Gemma decided to take out her fairy cards which had such beautiful pictures. Although they were lovely, she missed her tarot cards and had bought herself a new cheap set a few weeks ago and she still hadn't opened them. Gemma decided it was time to get them out of their packet and try a spread to see if things were changing. From the look of the cards, she was still not taking full responsibility for her life. Was it even possible for her to be the positive person Frank predicted, walking towards the sun? How could that reading have been right; with all the things she'd experienced over the last few months! It felt as if she was constantly challenged. Her sister used to refer to challenges as tests, but she was never sure about that. Whatever they were, it felt as if she was never going to get through them. Gemma was weary with life, which was something she didn't want to experience in her thirties!

As she looked at the tarot cards, Gemma noticed that whichever spread she laid out, the Justice card kept appearing. She very soon got bored and put the cards away. It was interesting, but not that relevant because it was more important to try and take control of her life. Being addicted to the cards wasn't healthy. She enjoyed messing around with them and discovering more about each of the meanings. It would take her years to get her head around all of them. Her telephone began ringing which quickly brought her out of her thoughts. She hastily packed her cards away and went to answer. To her surprise, it was Tony.

'Hi Gemma, I need to talk to you because I'm worried. I don't like what's happening to you lately, and I want you and the girls to come back and live here with me. It's not about us, I mean our relationship, it's about the girls and what's best for them. We don't have to sleep in the same room ...' his voice trailed off. Each word sounded to Gemma like a small explosion of anxiety! 'We can share the house and then look after the girls together. I think we'd have to tell other people we're back together because I'd want people to believe that we're a 'normal couple,' he continued anxiously.

Gemma was amazed. She didn't know what to say. She was speechless, and it wasn't often that she didn't have any words at all!

'Come back?' she finally managed to squeak out.

'Yes, Gem because you're not doing that well are you? Look at what's just happened. The girls seem all over the place. Lily isn't doing that well at school and Lacey doesn't really say much at all, does she? I think that there must be something the matter with her?'

Gemma went very silent. Living back with Tony was the last thing she wanted to do and why would she care what people thought! He obviously didn't understand her or her motives, but she didn't want to get into an argument with him. He was obviously concerned about them, but by going back to her old life, all their old problems would resurface. Gemma grabbed the edge of the chair and sat down with the telephone.

'We are divorced now Tony. How could we go back?

Gemma took a long deep breath, then said 'ok, I'll think about it.' Fortunately, Tony then dropped it but there was no way she would ever return to live with that man, but by saying this, she could temporarily get Tony off her back. Gemma needed time to recover her strength, and it felt as if Tony was making one final attempt to control her! Over the years she had learned the best way to handle him, and that was to back off slowly, rather than risk an onslaught! Gemma felt a little sorry for him, realising he was a little lonely. Despite his facade, did he still have feelings for her? He certainly wasn't going to admit it. Tony never expressed his feelings, which had been part of the problem. She remembered a token 'I love you' before having sex, but that was it. It never sounded genuine, more I expect this from you, so I'll go through the motions! The rest of the time, she felt lonely because he didn't take the time to bother listening to her. She sometimes felt alone now, but at least living with the girls, she had the freedom to enjoy her life the way she wanted. No, there was no going back, only moving forward. If she had been dancing the wrong dance so far, she had the opportunity to find the right dance now. She would learn the steps to take her forward. It was up to her. She would make her life, and it would be a good one.

ALESSANDRO

Alessandro lit a cigarette then turned on his computer. He noticed an email which said, if he continued to abuse women his protection couldn't be guaranteed. They knew that Alessandro had behaved foolishly with a woman called Sylvia which had led him into a great deal of trouble! The email also suggested it would be a wise idea if he left the United Kingdom as soon as possible and returned to Italy. They knew the woman he'd met worked in the legal profession and if he was investigated, it could make things difficult for both him and them. If he stayed where he was, he'd be placed behind bars. Alessandro quickly derived he had become a liability and the organisation were extremely unhappy with him. He was shocked that his drug suppliers knew his every move, but how? He decided that he wouldn't panic and it would be foolish to do a runner before the Court case even if it affected his income. He would be all right. He had other ways of earning money. He had to stay in England until this was over but after that Spain seemed his best option and he was continuing to look at properties there.

Alessandro planned to visit his father later today, which was another tricky situation. His Dad had moved from Italy to England shortly after his mother's death and was now living with a woman half his age, which Alessandro found embarrassing, so he avoided him as much as possible. He forced himself to visit him every month or so, but it was always a busy time, so he often left his father's house early as he had so little to say. He found it hard to forget how his dad treated him as a child, and it was doubtful that he ever would. Alessandro hated his father's new wife, if she was his wife. She was more likely his floozy. He'd never understood why they were together. She had to be a gold digger because she didn't appear to have much of a brain. His father often told the story about his prosperous vineyard in Italy, which went down well with women. They thought they'd travel with him and experience the good life, which he viewed as a bit of a joke!

Alessandro hated the old man, yet at the same time he was in awe of his ability to pull young women. At seventy years old, his father was still quite a charmer. He could give him some tips. He'd ask him if he wasn't so condescending!

Alessandro looked at the chart on which he was working. He'd learned how to produce astrology charts very quickly over the last couple of years. His mother had always been interested in astrology, and she'd taught him the basics as a child, but he'd never expected to have to use this knowledge. Life had a strange way of doing that to him. Several years ago, he'd bought an advanced computer program which produced charts quickly, which was a godsend in comparison to manually creating them by hand as his mother had. All he needed to know was the time, date, and place of birth of his clients. After a few months of doing this for his friends, while selling wine locally in Oxford, he gained an excellent reputation for astrology his local area. Alessandro soon acquired a fictional surname and began selling charts. It gave him enough cash to live on plus the opportunity to travel buy and sell drugs without suspicion. He'd been asked to have an inventive cover, so he found one! No-one knew who he was. People in Oxford knew him as Alessandro the Astrologer and Tarot reader and they assumed that he'd been doing that for years. He still sold a little wine to his old contacts in Italy which helped to boost his income. In the beginning, even he, regarded the astrology as a bit of a joke. He didn't want to take it too seriously, but as the months went on, he realised that he enjoyed doing the charts. Finding people's personality traits was fun and he found that he liked giving his clients guidance. He hoped that no-one would look too deeply into him because he was aware of his complexity. He had various identities which he used, dependant on where he was. He was always Alessandro the astrologer and tarot reader in England, but for his wine business, he always talked about his family from Tuscany. If you were Italian, you often had a family with a vineyard. He found the English were gullible, so white lying had become one of his skills. The only people who really knew him were Antonio because they were also involved with drugs. Alessandro soon got them interested when he realised how short of money they were, and they worked under him. He pulled them in from time to time to help him but it wasn't always necessary. They quickly showed up if they needed their fix, but they had still had to work for it. Alessandro discovered they weren't that dependable, too much cocaine over the years had done something to their brains. Half the time they didn't know what they were doing, but they proved to be good company at the odd dinner party. They knew a lot about animals, so the vet on television thing was believable. They were also good about persuading people to invest in his wine business which was an asset, and he needed investors if he was going to leave England permanently.

Alessandro laughed a little to himself. He loved living on the edge, and he considered it unlikely that any mud thrown at him by this Sylvia woman would stick. He found it hard to believe that she was a Barrister, although in hindsight, the situation was proving to be more challenging than he predicted. Sylvia was obviously no fool. He had been sure that he could handle it, despite the complications, because he'd been in many tricky situations over the years.

Alessandro met Sylvia on a train journey to London when he was travelling to meet his supplier. The woman was 'classy' and 'hot' and there was something mysterious about her. She appeared different from the other English women he'd met, because she was astute and she knew about wine! Sylvia was keen to chat to him. He recalled her mentioning the legal profession, but he assumed she was a junior solicitor, because she appeared so young. He obviously hadn't paid that much attention to the details at the time. He had perked up when she said she was looking for an investment of some kind. He then told her that he was looking for investors in his wine business which was a no-lose situation. She happily agreed to meet him later after their meetings in the city to hear about his business proposal over dinner. She explained it was something she rarely did, but they had both sensed a connection. Sylvia was sexually attracted to Alessandro within a short time of meeting him! He knew his sexuality was his hook, and he usually got what he wanted.

Alessandro went bankrupt a few years ago. The truth was, at one time in his life, he did have a thriving wine business in Italy. However, it wasn't at his family's vineyard. He had visited many vineyards and exported their wine. He was good at bending the truth. His business had taken a turn for the worse in the late nineties, when he was unexpectedly approached by a man dealing in cocaine. He was invited into their secret society which had many contacts not just in Italy, but throughout Europe. He desperately needed the money, and he wanted to start a new life, so Alessandro decided to take a chance. He had to get out of Italy and move to England, where there would be less heat on him, then he met up with their contacts in Oxford.

Alessandro soon rented a house and worked as an astrologer as a front. He knew it appeared a bizarre occupation, but as he didn't want people digging into his personal life, this allowed him another identity to throw people off the trail. His two worlds were quite different. He was an astrologer and tarot reader in addition to being a wine merchant and drug dealer. He now only supplied his friends with wine rather than businesses. Selling wine gave him a small income, and it was a cover for the goods he delivered. Astrology gave him some breathing space. It was never meant to be, or was it, he wondered? He enjoyed being the astrologer because it felt like the real him. However, the money he made from the drugs went into his Italian bank account. He planned to return to Italy to buy his own vineyard which had been his dream for many years. Alessandro was surprised at how little money he made in comparison with people who were higher up in the organisation. He occasionally got the opportunity to make big money, but this was rare as time went on. His superiors told him what price to buy and sell, and there was no freedom of choice. Men were controlling him further up the network that he'd never met. He often felt scared and wished that he was only Alessandro the astrologer. Living a double life was both exhausting and confusing. He would often wake up in the morning and wonder who and where he was! He'd planned to get out of selling drugs a few years ago when he discovered that he really enjoyed astrology. Unfortunately, while he was at a dinner in Oxford, someone must have known of his whereabouts and made him another offer he couldn't refuse. Money and drugs had become an addiction to him. Despite this, he still planned to get out as soon as he had enough to buy a decent property. Unfortunately, things kept getting in the way, particularly situations with women!

Alessandro had to have women. They were his only relief from stress. They were like a drug to him. He was used to getting his way. Although his father had been cruel to him as a child, he had been his mother's favourite. Alessandro was the youngest of four boys and his mother adored him. She'd died in a tragic accident in the late eighties which had torn him apart because she was the only woman who had given him love. Alessandro wanted to be loved but he didn't know how to receive. His father was a cold unaffectionate man who was seldom around. He rarely smiled at his family and he had an awful temper. He also drank heavily. Alessandro had often found him lying on the floor early in the morning. He'd gone to sleep wherever he finished his previous night's bottle. Alessandro's life was intolerable when his father was at home. He found it incredible that his parents ran a vineyard. His father was gone most of the day, while his mother did the chores. His father usually returned most evenings with two bottles of wine and started to become abusive after dinner. Alessandro and his brothers were then sent up to their room, a small bedroom in an old Italian farmhouse and told not to make any noise.

The children were left upstairs for hours on end. They were often not allowed downstairs until the following morning when their father had gone to work. Alessandro was happy when his father left the house because he could spend some time with his mother, but he dreaded his return because if his father saw his mother giving him, or his brothers attention, he'd become angry. He told her she was spoiling them.

Alessandro's mother tried awfully hard to be a normal loving mother, but most of the time it was impossible. After the accident, Alessandro never allowed himself the time to grieve her death, and for a long time after her funeral, he felt the influence of his father's misery which felt like a dark shadow on him.

When Alessandro was old enough, he started working at a nearby vineyard, which was an escape from home and a few years later he began selling the wine. Alessandro soon found he was good at selling, and things started to go well for him. He made new friends. He had his own money and a room in a small nearby town. However, after the economic boom of the eighties, the nineties proved to be challenging. People were turning to hypermarkets for their wine. They came over from the United Kingdom by the carload to places like Boulogne to buy up cheap French wine. This left him struggling to make a living, even though the wine he sold was far superior. Alessandro knew there was no comparison, but the public was more interested in price than quality.

Taking Sylvia out to dinner and persuading her to invest in his business, had been a huge mistake. He felt annoyed at himself for not finding out more about her. Although on meeting Sylvia, it was obvious that she was well travelled having spent time in Italy, Spain, and France, and she appeared extremely interested in new opportunities. With his knowledge of Italian wine, he concluded that it would be easy to impress her. For a ten-thousand-pound investment, he promised her a ten per cent return in the first year, and within five years she would double her money. He explained it was a no-lose situation, and it didn't take him long to draw up a contract and mock up some figures to make his business appear profitable! Sylvia ran the numbers past her accountant, who agreed it seemed a reasonable investment, but her accountant had little knowledge of wine. Alessandro originally intended to boost his business with money he'd received from drugs, but it wasn't always easy to find a decent supply, and he had to settle for an inferior version, so his sales dropped. He knew if he passed it off for something it wasn't, his life would be taking too great a risk. In the meantime, Sylvia had done some checking up on him and discovered that his business wasn't the successful company she was led to believe. Alessandro felt his only choice was to alter the wording in the contract and wing it until he sorted out his financial mess.

Fortunately, Sylvia had left her signed copy of the contract with him, which enabled him to edit both documents. He then returned the contract to her in the post. It now read something a little different to what was agreed and her profits were open-ended. If the document was examined by the court, Alessandro doubted it would get past the scrutiny of the Judge, which worried him.

Alessandro calculated that he only needed a few more thousand to get out of the drug business permanently. He decided it was better to forget the idea of buying a vineyard in Italy, because he wanted to start again somewhere new. There was a place in the Spanish Sierra Nevada Mountains which looked ideal, and the location was excellent. He'd take early retirement and sell the rest of his wine to the locals. There was no way he planned to stay in drug dealing when it was so dangerous. He wanted to become a full-time astrologer and reader, creating astrology charts for the locals. He spoke fluent Spanish, so the transition would be smooth, and it would take the pressure off! His main problem now, was he was considered a risky investment. Since he tried to get money out of the Barrister woman, he'd become a liability. His drug suppliers knew that Alessandro had left a trail of unhappy women behind him, some of which had made allegations against him. Fortunately for him, so far, none of their claims had held up. Then there was Susie who was being difficult, insisting that he was the father of her child, but for all he knew, she could have had several lovers! He wanted to finish their association before anything else happened, but she'd now involved her parents.

Alessandro scanned through the paper and saw that there were one or two mind body soul events that he could attend. One near Oxford, and another was on the coast, near Southampton. It wouldn't bring in that much, a couple of hundred pounds but it would be something, and he was desperate. If the events worked out, they would pay for his flight to Spain to check out this villa. When he made enquiries about it, he discovered it had been on the market for a couple of years, and recently the price had dropped, so he needed to go soon. It was too remote for most people, as it didn't have a proper transport system, but he didn't care because it would be perfect for what he wanted, an escape.

RENEWED ENERGY

The sun shone through the cottage windows, and Gemma felt better. She no longer ached. Today, she was taking Lacey clothes shopping because Lily had gone to her friend's house for the full day. Gemma was pleased to be spending some time with Lacey because she needed a little one to one time with her eldest daughter. It would be great for them both. Lacey was tall and slim, and most of her clothes looked baggy, so she had taken to wearing leggings with long tops.

They soon arrived in the local town and started working their way through the shops. Lacey had her own opinions about what she liked, which Gemma didn't mind because she thought it was great that her daughter had a mind of her own. She let her lead the way and tried not to comment on the price unless it was way out of her budget. In the end, Lacey bought a pair of black leggings and a long black top with an unusual ethnic design. This surprised Gemma, because she thought it was more like something that she'd wear, but Lacey seemed delighted with her purchase, so she didn't comment. Gemma smiled at her daughter. Lacey was growing up very quickly, and she appeared happy today. For once, they had the time to stroll and enjoy the sun together.

Gemma picked up a local newspaper and headed towards the cafe where she worked. She didn't work on Saturdays, but it was one of their busiest days, and it was packed with customers. The Saturday staff seemed genuinely pleased to see her and Lacey, although Margery said that if they sat there for too long, she'd put them both to work! Gemma just laughed because Margery was always teasing her. Although they were extremely busy today, they had enough staff working.

Lacey took out her mobile phone and decided to play a game while Gemma drank her coffee. She opened her newspaper to look at the what's on-page. As soon as she started to read, she noticed on the following Sunday, there was a Mind Body and Soul event on the coast near Southampton. It also gave a contact number for stallholders who were interested in having a table. Gemma thought she might ring and ask if she could offer Tarot Readings, but she wasn't sure if she wanted to travel that far. She folded the paper and spoke to Lacey.

'Come on Lacey, we'd better get going because by the time we get home, it'll be lunchtime and I need to make a few phone calls.'

Lacey turned off the game and stood up. Gemma noticed that she was in a much better mood since they had bought her some new clothes! When Lily was around, they often competed for attention. Lacey loved it when her sister saw a friend for the entire day, and she wished it would happen more often! Gemma knew this, but she only had one pair of hands and at times she felt split down the middle! She loved both her girls and she wanted to give them as much time as possible, but with work and everything else, it often proved impossible.

They drove home and unpacked their purchases, and it wasn't long before the girls were chilled out in front of the television. Gemma decided to give Jo her riding friend a quick call.

'Hi Jo, have you got time to come over tonight. I need to practice my readings because I'm thinking of doing an event next week. There will be lots of readers there, but I thought I might try and get a table.'

'Well, I'm busy right now, because I've been at the stables all day and I've got to take a shower and get changed. I've started training as a riding instructor. It's full on but I absolutely love it. I'm always out! I can pop over for an hour tonight. Is that long enough?' Jo replied.

After dinner, Gemma took out her cards and gave Jo a reading. Her friend was surprised how accurate Gemma was, because she'd revealed some of her past, present and future. Gemma was also astounded by the speed the answers came to her. Was she fine tuning her gift? It was exciting!

'Spooky,' said Jo, then she laughed. 'I'm only joking, it was excellent. I can relate to what you are saying. You ought to give the event a shot Gem, why not? You could do with the money, and then you'll be able to come riding with me again. It's been a month now, hasn't it? What happened to that Italian guy you were seeing or was he Spanish? Weird accent but he was obviously well-travelled. I saw a clip of him on YouTube when I was looking up astrology readings. He didn't look like your typical astrologer to me. He looked smart, more like a businessperson. What happened to him then? I thought you were going over to his house for dinner?' Jo persisted.

Gemma didn't want to talk about Alessandro. She'd spent the last month trying to get him out of her head and she didn't want to hear his name again! She was often shaky when she thought about him, but over the last few weeks it had become a lot better. She decided to keep it brief!

'I went for dinner at his house and while I was there, I found a letter from a young woman, saying she was the mother of his child! I questioned him about it, but he never gave me a straight answer, so I decided to give him a wide berth.'

'Really?' answered Jo. 'Men, they always have something to hide! If only they would be upfront from the beginning,' she replied, looking a little surprised.

'I'm concentrating on myself and the girls now. I took Lacey shopping today, and we had a fun time. I'm not interested in having a relationship. Not anytime soon. To be honest, I'm perfectly happy on my own.'

'I never understood why you left Tony. I know he wasn't perfect, but at least you were financially secure. I saw him last week. I bumped into him at that cafe down by the river, not the one where you work, the other one. We had a quick chat. He seemed completely stressed out. He was never like that when you were with him. He mumbled something about being bogged down with work. He has an awful court case coming up in the next few weeks. The strain certainly showed, poor guy. Are you sure you don't want to go back with him? I always thought you two were soul mates. Every relationship has difficulties, but surely you could have worked through them. He's always polite and jokey with me. I sometimes thought dating him could be fun!' Jo continued.

'Well, forgive me for saying so Jo, but you have no idea how controlling Tony is. I could go back tomorrow, but nothing would change. I was doing absolutely everything, and he was obsessed with his work. He never made the time for the girls or me, and I don't see how that would ever change when he's taking on more work!' Gemma felt annoyed by Jo's attitude and she hoped this was the end of the conversation. She didn't need her friend taking Tony's side, and not seeing things from her perspective!

'Have you looked at the cards yourself?' asked Jo as she tactfully tried to change the subject.

'Yes of course I have, but I try not too because it's considered unlucky to read for yourself. I could start living my life like the couple at the bus stop who made all their decisions by consulting the tarot.

'What couple at the bus stop? Oh Gem, you've gone around the bend with all your weird stuff! I'm only joking but please, no dark secrets. What's coming up for you,' asked Jo, who clearly didn't want to let this go!

'It's no dark secret Jo. I'm happy to tell you what's coming up for me. Justice,' replied Gemma, smiling.

'Ah, about time,' replied Jo.

GEMMA'S FIRST EVENT

It was a warm Sunday in May. The birds were singing, and daisies were poking their heads through the grass. The shrubs were growing rapidly, and the sky was clear. It was a perfect spring day, but Gemma thought the nights were sometimes chilly. Today she wore a long loose patterned skirt, natural colour leather sandals and a long brown cardigan with a little cream scoop neck top and various necklaces. Gemma knew that she looked attractive, and she was happy with her appearance. Although the girls were busy getting ready to go to their fathers, they still both noticed how nice their Mum looked.

'You look smart Mum; you must be going somewhere?' asked Lacey.

Gemma told them that she was going to work at a healing fair, but she would be back before their father dropped them off. The girls said goodbye and went out to their father's car smiling and chatting. He'd planned to take them to Bristol Zoo for a day out, and they seemed excited. Everything was working out well, and Gemma felt relieved.

When Gemma arrived at the mind body soul event, she had forty-five minutes to spare, which was plenty of time to set up her stand and get into a calm space. She hoped she could pull this off. It was all right getting messages at home when it was quiet, but with a lot of activity around her, that was different. She was concerned that she'd be unable to hear a thing! Her friend Jo had said that she'd try and pop in late afternoon. At least there would be a familiar face to encourage her. Gemma spread out her cloth on the wooden table. The fabric was made of gold and silver material which was very silky, and it looked stunning. By the time she'd laid out several crystals, some fresh flowers and her cards, everything seemed to spring to life. Gemma decided to give people a choice, they could pick either tarot or angel cards. She'd decided to go with the flow and forget about expectations! In fact, even if she took nothing, it would be okay because it was her first-ever event, so she thought it was vital for her to gain experience.

Gemma noticed that some of the other people had boards with their names displayed on them. A few also had photographs, and some of them were smaller, which stood up on their own. She hadn't really thought about having her name or a price, but it seemed obvious now. Fortunately, she had some white card, felt tip pens and sticky tape. There was a big blank space on the wall behind her to place a sign. The hall was a charming bright modern building, and there was plenty of space. She thought initially that this was a tiny event, but she soon discovered that there were fifty stallholders. Gemma had stand twenty-five, and she loved her stand because it was a corner which meant that she had some privacy for her readings. Gemma enthusiastically climbed on to her chair to attach her notice to the wall. If she had it high above her head, then hopefully people would see it as they came in. It was bold, so it would be visible. Her readings were going to be short, and she was charging ten pounds. As she stretched up with the notice in one hand, and sticky tack in the other, she suddenly heard a voice she recognised behind her.

'Gemma what are you doing here?' she heard someone say, as she slowly turned around to see Alessandro standing just a few feet away, peering up her skirt! She was horrified. Gemma knew he did events but thought it unlikely that he would travel this far. It had crossed her mind a couple of days ago that there was a slim possibility, but she never dreamt she would see him again.

'I'm sticking up a notice,' Gemma replied as she hastily got down from the chair. There was no way Alessandro was going to upset her. She'd looked forward to giving readings for months and she certainly wasn't going to let him get the better of her. There had to be a way of seeing Alessandro without him completely ruining her day. The last thing she wanted to do was to look like a fool.

'Gemma, I have a clever idea. I could be your pimp and arrange for us to sleep with couples for money. What do you think?' said Alessandro as he surveyed her body.

Gemma turned and quickly walked away. She had to leave the hall as fast as possible and take some long deep breaths. Alessandro made her feel sick. She needed fresh air, coffee, or both. Why didn't she just run to her car and head home? She could not believe what he said. The man must be sick, she thought to herself. He may well appear charming and be brilliant at astrology, but Gemma knew there was a whole host of dark energy that was lurking underneath! She hoped no-one would ask if she knew him, because if they did, she would find it difficult not to tell the truth. But she was afraid and embarrassed. Besides, who would believe her when everyone thought he was terrific!

Gemma stood in the car park breathing in deeply as she hastily swigged her coffee. She still had plenty of time. She could see Alessandro was talking to the event organiser and his behaviour appeared a little aggressive. He then went to sit down at his table which to Gemma's horror, was next to hers! She strode back to her stand and noticed that there was at least some space in between them. Not a lot of space though, she thought, but a breathing space. She'd have to focus on holding her own energy and not be influenced by him. It was enormously challenging. Was she strong enough to do it?

Alessandro suddenly leaned across the gap. 'Gemma, you're sitting at the wrong table. That's my table. You should have this one, twenty-four because I always sit in the southeastern corner. It's good Feng Shui, so you'll have to move.'

Liberty Angel

Gemma couldn't believe it. She'd just finished setting everything up, and her cards were laid out on the table. She could feel her heart beating as she tried to steady herself.

'I'm not going anywhere,' she hissed.

Alessandro turned his head away, and Gemma noticed that he appeared shocked at not getting his own way!

As Gemma's day progressed, she became busy and she hardly noticed Alessandro. He held far less importance and was practically invisible! At one time, people were queuing to have readings with her, and she had her work cut out focusing on her clients.

Surprisingly, Alessandro was not terribly busy. When she got up for a coffee, she saw that he was printing off astrology charts and taking three tarot cards for each person. She heard him pack up early while she still had two people on her list.

'Fantastic, I love your openness and honesty. If there's one thing I can't stand, it's when people give you a load of flannel. Thank you for your guidance. Your reading was so helpful. It was spot on,' her lady said, as she left.

Gemma was pleased she could help, and her confidence was building. She also had a promotion at the cafe. Things were certainly looking up. She thought about Frank and what he'd said about being invisible, and she realised that it was a matter of choice. Someone could upset her if she let them, but if she didn't want to take it on board, she could zone out. It was a matter of tuning in or out. She could see the physical outline of

151

Alessandro when he was leaning close, but as she threw herself into her work and focused on her intention, he had little influence. She also thought about what Adrian taught her during Buddhist meditation classes. He'd often said, 'if it isn't possible to alter our circumstances, we can still change our reaction to those things.' Gemma realised how true this was. She'd coped well today, and she was extremely pleased with herself. Besides, there was now a small pile of money to spend on the girls or she could buy something for her. She might take them to see the film they had been nagging about for weeks! Alessandro had become a blot on the horizon, and he no longer held any energy over her.

Gemma randomly turned a tarot card over for herself. JUSTICE had appeared again. Then she picked an angel card which surprisingly said FREEDOM, which she found extremely interesting. Was she living through the cards, or were the energies of the cards living through her?

BACK AT HOME

Tony brought the children back home to Gemma. He was relieved because he loved having the girls, but he needed to get on with his work. He hardly had time to eat lately. He hadn't received a response from Gemma about them getting back together, so he assumed she wasn't interested. Was she going somewhere today? He was frustrated that he didn't know what she was up to. He'd noticed significant changes in her behaviour. The way she dressed was different, and she appeared more confident. He had to admit he felt more attracted to her now, than when he was married to her! He wished he had never started this dating thing because some of these women behaved more strangely than Gemma ever had! The dating scene was different than he imagined. What he wanted was a woman who was independent, but still an excellent cook and homemaker. He didn't have time for cooking or keeping the house tidy, because he was always up to his eyes in legal cases which were taking over his life!

Sylvia Jones' case was proving to be particularly challenging and took up way too much time. Fortunately, he had quite a bit of evidence now. The police had gone through their files and found several complaints from women about his behaviour. There was no doubt that Alessandro had been warned a few times about his behaviour with women, and there was a court case where he had been acquitted, but the fraud thing was hard to prove. The man had a good accountant, and there appeared to be nothing the matter with the figures. Alessandro could repay the returns on the investment because his wine business was doing quite well. Despite this, Sylvia expected to receive higher dividends than she was getting and she'd received none so far! There was something wrong somewhere! It didn't add up. It was also comical that the man was posing as an astrologer. A hobby yes, but to go out and make money from it. That was a joke.

Alessandro had his fingers in all sorts of pies but making sense of it was something else! Tony decided to use evidence from a prior accusation of sexual assault. He knew that dragging up an old case was risky because the Judge could dismiss it, but in the absence of anything better he had little choice. Tony needed to demonstrate that this man had a bad reputation with women, as well as his engagement in shady business dealings. Alessandro would no doubt end up having to pay back the amount Sylvia invested in his business, plus damages, the usual scenario. But proving Alessandro's behaviour was unprofessional, and his client had been misinformed was challenging. He knew the main issue was the contract which Sylvia claimed was different to the one she signed. It was strange that she signed it because a woman with her ability would have gone through it with a fine-toothed comb. Unless his client had been drunk, then it was entirely possible that Sylvia may have fallen for this womaniser, despite her denial.

Tony felt tired. He took off his glasses and rubbed his eyes. Things were so much easier when Gemma had been around for support. He hadn't involved her in any of his cases, but her hugs and meals had been helpful. He had a meeting with Sylvia this afternoon. He was relieved that he managed to find her a suitable barrister. The paperwork needed to go to chambers today, and there was certainly a stack of it! One or two things had still to be examined. One of them was obvious, did they have a sexual relationship? He didn't want to go this route, but with Alessandro's history with women it had become necessary to ask these questions.

Sylvia sat in the upstairs of an old antiquated legal office which had seen better days. It smelled slightly musty, which began to irritate the back of her throat. She was familiar with Tony's office, having gone there many times to have documents sworn. Her days of a junior Solicitor were long gone, but somehow the office looked brighter and more promising then, not old, and lacklustre, as it did now! The room could easily be improved with a lick of paint and some flowers to bring the old place back to life, she thought.

Sylvia spent a large amount of time in London over the last few years. She'd been involved in some very significant cases, and she deeply missed her work. If only she could get these proceedings out of the way, she could get on with her life. This was the last straw, after a run of unfortunate events. The first, was the bullying her daughter experienced at boarding school, which had been an ongoing problem. Sylvia felt bitterly disappointed because it was a good school that she'd attended, so she hoped Beth would take to the school as she had. To her disappointment there had been nothing but trouble since her daughter started. It wasn't Beth's fault. The girls teased her about her appearance because she had a mild disability. It was hardly noticeable, but these girls were cruel. Teenage girls had to look like movie stars nowadays to be accepted! Her daughter didn't meet that criteria and never would. Pupils were taken out of the school by their parents because they were anorexic. They had been known to starve themselves to look like supermodels; at least her daughter didn't do that. Things were complicated enough with her career, without all the school problems particularly after she lost a case at the Old Bailey, which would have meant a win not just for her client, but for women in general. Sometimes she hated the legal system. Despite current legislation; she'd seen such inequality. Sylvia felt pushed from pillar to post, and now this. She heard the whispers about her private life, and she didn't need the insult of being ripped off by this petty wine merchant. There were awful looks, pretend coughs and heads turning amongst her colleagues. God damn it, was it worth it. Now her daughter was suffering. Could things get any worse?

Sylvia turned to Tony, who quickly read through the case notes, underlining the things that needed to be explained to the Court.

'Good afternoon, Sylvia. I've been examining the case. I apologise for asking you this, but I need it for the record. Was Alessandro's behaviour towards you in any way inappropriate?' questioned Tony, who shuffled in his chair, appearing slightly uncomfortable.

Sylvia stared at Tony. It was one of her long hard looks that she was accustomed to using in court. What was he talking about? Of course she didn't have sex with Alessandro. Why would Tony think that? He was very charming, but he wasn't on her level. She may well have been tempted at one stage in the evening because there was an attraction, but when he mentioned he was being harassed by several women, it was clear to her that he had a problem with his ego!

Sylvia felt ashamed that she'd agreed to sign the contract, but she always honoured her word. It was a business meeting, not a date, so what was Tony asking? Alessandro thought she was genuinely interested in his wine business. Was Tony assuming that she dived into bed with any man she came across! After a long deep breath, she stared back at him.

'Tony, we discussed business together. I've already explained to you that I met the man on a train to London. We also met a few times in Oxford so that I could collect some bottles of wine for potential customers. I was investing in his business. It had nothing to do with sex. To be honest, I feel a bit insulted. The man promised that I would have a great return on my investment which I considered to be small at the time. Certainly nothing like my daughter's school fees! Do you think I would be that stupid to sign a contract which is that open-ended? It's obviously been tampered with. Alessandro sent it to me in the post a few weeks after I'd signed it and I didn't recheck the document, which I realise now was an oversight. I have no idea when or how he did it, but I know he changed the terms. I also know it was foolish of me to sign it in the first place, but forgery is a crime. I need you to dig deep Tony. Alessandro pretends to be a simple man, but he's not. He's extremely devious. I'm sure that he has many dealings in different organisations,' explained Sylvia, sounding annoyed.

'That may well be the case Sylvia, but we can only work with the facts and unfortunately, what we do have is a contract signed by you. It could appear to the Jury that you signed the contract without reading it properly, under the influence of alcohol and you then left it behind!'

Tony felt embarrassed that he stated the facts so brutally, but Sylvia would experience this in Court, or even worse. If his client had drunk several glasses of wine with Alessandro that evening and ended up in his hotel room, that was one thing, but any mention of it would make her look foolish. This was something he wanted to avoid. She'd obviously made a bad investment when she was vulnerable. He'd been told that Sylvia had been under a lot of strain lately, something about her daughter having a tough time at school. Sylvia had taken time out from her work. He doubted Alessandro amended the contract due to consequences, but he couldn't be sure so he would have to leave that one to the Judge! Tony felt relieved that this case had been passed to the Barrister. He wanted to go home and get this stuff out of his head. It made him angry that a man could behave in this way. He hated everything he represented. Alessandro was a womaniser, cheat, and fraud. Even worse, he was posing as an astrologer and making money from it, which was ludicrous. How did he get away with it? Thankfully, his world was about to come crashing down, and people would soon discover the truth!

GEMMA

The girls had gone up to bed, and Gemma was resting with her feet up, which was a rare occurrence because she seldom stopped. Her employer had recently given her a promotion with a slight pay rise, so Gemma decided to open a bottle of Australian white wine and take some time to relax. The television annoyed her, but the book she was reading on angels was fascinating. Gemma also read about orbs, and she now realised what had made the round light in the hospital and other places. It was definitely some kind of visitation. She hoped it was angelic. This made sense to her because it had always happened when she was vulnerable. At last, she was beginning to get on top of things, and she felt emotionally stable. The girls were happy, and there was more money for them. Not a fortune, but enough to stop her worrying. Gemma had also made a few new friends, and she wasn't so lonely, so everything had begun to fall into place. When her phone rang unexpectedly, Gemma jumped a mile! Her phone seldom rang, and never at nine in the evening, so it made her jump. As soon as she heard the Italian accent, she knew who it was, and felt shocked. Why would Alessandro phone her after their last incident? Gemma thought he understood that she never wanted to see him again.

'Hello Gemma, I'm warning you not to talk to anyone about what happened between us. I don't need it right now. If I hear that you've been talking to anyone, I'll know about it and I'll make your life hell.'

Gemma opened her mouth to say something to Alessandro but found that nothing came out. She then started to shake, so she quickly hung up and poured herself a glass of wine. Was Alessandro threatening her? He was warning her to keep quiet. She should go straight to the Police and tell them the truth? She knew it was the best thing to do, but the thought of it was terrifying. As she lived alone, she couldn't risk anything happening to her or the girls, so for the time being she'd ignore his phone calls. Why couldn't he just go away and stay away. The man was obviously nuts! Gemma took out the astrology chart Alessandro had created for her and checked his predictions for the coming year. Surprisingly, he'd written that she would have a relationship which would prove to be traumatic and was better left alone. It would go on for several months, and then this person would disappear as if they'd never existed. Gemma looked at the words again. It was strange how they jumped out as if it was a message for her. She decided to centre her energy. She knew how to breathe deeply and bring her awareness back to the present moment. It was something that she'd learned in Buddhist meditation. She was determined that Alessandro wouldn't wreck her life. She was a free woman, and she could do what she wanted. No man was going to threaten her. How dare he? She hated Alessandro with every cell in her body. Forgiving people like him was hard. Talking about it was one thing, but doing it was different. Why do 'spiritual people' keep using this word when they have absolutely no idea what it means? Do any of them know just how hard it is to forgive? If she could forgive him for what he did to her, then maybe she could let both him and John go and it would be easier for her to move on. She was angry and punched a cushion. Then she had an idea. She decided to hit a pillow for Tony, John, and Alessandro. She had three different ones lined up on the sofa. First, she would punch the hell out of Tony, then John and last of all she would really go for it and finish off Alessandro! Gemma was surprised at how hard she could punch. This would have worked well when she had been bullied at school! Gemma whacked all three cushions in turn and began to enjoy herself! When she'd finished and her arms began to ache, she chucked them in a pile on the floor, then sat on them and cried. Tears of exhaustion and disappointment kept coming until she had no tears left.

Gemma woke in the early hours of the morning with something gently brushing her face. She must have left the window open because she could feel warm air as if it was blowing on her. Her eyelids flickered then she gradually opened them and saw the outline of a huge white angel. The angel was standing at the foot of her bed. The love which came from the angel was overwhelming. Gemma felt a warm glow of pure love. It was as if the angel was watching her and sending her love. She kept very still but she wasn't afraid. She reached her hands out from under the covers, to find they were submerged in white feathers! There was a sense of timelessness and ultimate peace. She must have laid there for about five minutes rejuvenating before she moved. Then unexpectedly, she heard the door creak open and there stood Lacey, she was already dressed for school, and she was smiling.

'Hello Mum, surprise! I've brought you a cup of tea and some toast.' Gemma was amazed. This had never happened before, but they had become closer since their last shopping trip. Gemma's eyes suddenly filled with tears. She'd been stupid. She had so much love for her children; she didn't need anyone else in her life. She lifted her head to say thank you and pulled Lacey towards her to give her a hug. She was full of love. Her daughter, who obviously sensed something different about her, smiled back. Lacey then went to wake her sister up, while Gemma continued to lay there astounded!

ALESSANDRO

Alessandro put down the phone. He'd received a letter from his Solicitor to say that his court case was coming up in the next few weeks, and he had a top Barrister on his case. The bitch Sylvia was throwing everything at him she could find. It was crazy that she would spend all this energy going after him, when if she waited, he would refund her investment. It was only ten thousand pounds. He could make that in one job if he got the right buyer for his cocaine. His Barrister had already told him that it was unlikely Sylvia could prove to the Court that he didn't intend making the payments. The contract was open-ended, which meant the profits Sylvia would receive had no time limit stamped on them. She would receive them as and when he was able to send them. If she had misunderstood this, then she hadn't properly understood the contract.

Alessandro had also been informed, that if he had any skeletons in the closet, it would be wise to reveal them now. It was his last opportunity to get his story straight before they went to Court. His Solicitor considered that the sexual assault charge from a woman a few years ago was no longer an issue. Still, anything could happen, especially if he'd been indiscreet.

'Indiscreet,' thought Alessandro. How the English made him laugh. It wasn't a question of being discreet! If he wanted a woman, he wanted a woman, provided she didn't complain too much. That's what he'd always done. Still, he didn't need anyone finding out about his love child. If it became known that he had abandoned Susie, it wouldn't do him any favours, especially with her being a student!

Alessandro took out his passport. He remembered what his Solicitor had told him, about how running would be a terrible idea, with the court case being so close. He would have to stay in England and avoid any trips to Italy, even if it was to spend time with friends. He hated this because he felt like a caged animal. His charts were piled up around him on his desk. There was also a new letter from Susie asking if she could call by and see him to talk about things. He knew what this meant. What she was saying was she wanted more money. He begrudgingly wrote out another cheque for two hundred pounds this time. He scribbled a note to say that he'd see her at the end of the month. He couldn't cope with seeing her now, and deal with going to Court. If Sylvia won which was doubtful, he might get away with paying the ten thousand back and court fees, but he'd been warned that in addition, he'd have to pay Sylvia damages on top. It could cripple him. His funds were low, and he still had his eye keenly set on the villa in Spain. The price had dropped further, so it was a suitable time for him to buy. He knew that as soon as the court case hit the papers, he wouldn't be able to attend anymore events. He was running dry, and the wine wasn't flowing either because he'd had very few orders lately. Sometimes the University bar took a few bottles, but they were no longer interested. He'd have to chase his friends and see if he could get some money in the bank. One thing was for sure, he wasn't going near any drugs because it was too risky now.

Alessandro looked at his computer. He'd already closed his email account, but then opened a fresh one. His previous account had emails on there, which could lead back to his suppliers. If that happened, he'd be gone! He knew how dangerous this work was when he took it on. Many of his past contacts had disappeared. He wasn't sure if they'd gone quiet because something happened to them or if they'd just moved away but he never found out the truth! Drug dealing with these people was dangerous but at the time he had no choice. He soon regretted getting involved. He longed to be the man he set out to be when he moved to England, Alessandro the astrologer. If only he'd listened to his mother. 'Alessandro, she'd told him, never owe a man anything, and make sure that he owes you nothing, and all will be well.'

His mother was a wise woman. His dad, on the other hand, was a tyrant and bully who continually abused her. He'd always wanted to be like his mother, kind and gentle, but he knew that part of him was like his father. He just couldn't help himself. He'd tried therapy in Italy for his personality disorder, but it was a waste of time. He'd not stuck at it. He found it easier to have different identities, so he could hide behind them. Some of them were ones he dreamed of as a child. If he used a different name and became someone else, he felt free. He could be himself when he was not himself!

Deep down, Alessandro knew that he had no self-love. He believed he was a copy of his father who he hated. After several years of living alone, his dad moved to England. Alessandro told his friends that his parents lived around the corner rather than having the hassle of explaining his mother's tragic death. Alessandro knew that his mother would be ashamed of him now. Why had he been so weak? He wanted to turn his life around selling wine. It was hardly his fault that he ran into difficulties when he couldn't match the price of the hypermarkets. On reflection, it was madness going to live in Oxford, near his father who was the person he wanted to get away from, but without moving there he would never have had the opportunity to earn more money in a month than most people would see in a year! It was also something that he could never talk about or share with friends. Some months later, he discovered that Antonio and Rosie were already involved. He often wondered if they had set up his meeting from the start. It always felt bizarre how he ran into these people. He'd never been to his friends fictional animal shelter, nor seen the television program they talked about. It was a bunch of lies. Sometimes they asked him for cocaine when they couldn't get hold of any. They'd asked a lot lately, but he didn't have anything, not even crack. They seemed moody and annoyed at him. In recent months they'd only wanted to visit when he was putting on a dinner, so they could take what was on offer. He was sick of them.

Alessandro walked to the local shops to buy a packet of cigarettes and a newspaper. On his return, he gasped as he noticed two pictures. One was on a trip to Italy a couple of years ago, and the other was of him around the age of ten. He had no idea how the newspaper got hold of the pictures. Did the people he worked for dig them up or was it his father. Nothing would surprise him! The old git would do anything for money, including shopping his own son. The people he worked for must want him out of the way, or even dead because he might inadvertently expose them. He'd become a liability, because he wasn't earning any money for them. Surely, he'd be better off in jail than knocked off by them, or something worse! Fear engulfed him, and his heart began to race. How could something that started so casually change into this nightmare? His mind flashed back to the train and the bitch Sylvia. For all he knew, she could have been put there as well! The whole thing could be a set up to make him fall. Why didn't she just talk to him about the money instead of going the legal route? Yes, it was a pain that he'd have to pay her back, but anything was better than this.

Fortunately, his solicitor was convinced that there wasn't anything else to come out of the woodwork, so he'd just have to keep his fingers crossed. He'd wiped everything clean from his computer. He was now an astrologer and part-time wine merchant. He went upstairs and looked for a decent suit and tie. Alessandro had been advised that if he dressed smartly, it could help him, but he was still worried. He'd discovered that Saturn had a strong influence in his chart right now, which meant anything could happen!

GEMMA

Gemma had already taken the children to school and she planned to cut the grass before she left for work. Everything looked beautiful outside, and it made her forget about what was said in the horrific telephone call, a couple of nights ago. The thought of it made her feel sick, so she needed to focus on getting on with things. She'd started seeing a local counsellor and hypnotherapist, someone she knew had a good reputation and could trust. Yesterday she'd found the courage to tell Marion about Alessandro. She'd explained how she first met him and what happened to her on that awful night in Oxford. Gemma could no longer keep it a secret. It was tearing her apart, and she had to be strong for the girls. She felt relieved that at last, she had someone to talk too.

Marion looked very intently at Gemma. 'Everything you say to me is completely confidential Gemma but you must speak out about this. What you're telling me is illegal. The man raped you, and he must suffer the consequences. If you don't want to do it for you, then do it for the other women. I'm sure that you are not the only woman who has been in this position. This man could have abused many women, and he's been allowed to get away with it.'

Gemma thought things through. She hadn't even considered that Alessandro may have behaved the same way to other women. It now dawned on her that this was a strong possibility. She loathed the man and felt anger rising inside her. He was a risk to any woman in his company, and he needed stopping.

Gemma continued to cut the grass vigorously. It was looking lovely now. She wanted to trim around the edges and put some flowers in hanging baskets. She tried to clear Alessandro from her mind, so she made a coffee and sat down to read the newspaper. Gemma turned the page, gasped, and nearly dropped her coffee. The paper said that a well-known barrister was bringing charges against this wine merchant for deception and fraud. The case was at the Crown Court on the twenty eighth of June. The Solicitor who represented Miss Jones said that these were severe allegations, and she hoped there would be justice. Miss Jones is hoping to return to work after the court case, which has caused her considerable stress and anxiety.'

Whoever Miss Jones was, she'd obviously suffered at the hands of Alessandro too. Gemma couldn't believe what she was reading, but it had to be him because there was a photograph of him on the third page. She made a note of the date in her diary. She felt terrible. Even though this man was no longer in her life he still managed to upset her. She sat on the sofa and put on some relaxing music. She needed to meditate and regain her balance! As soon as she closed her eyes, she felt a connection to something, but she wasn't sure what. As she continued to breathe, she felt a vast column of light come into her body from the crown of her head. Gemma felt as if she was growing taller, as a powerful energy from a limitless being engulfed her. It lifted her head, and she could feel her physical shape alter. She quickly glanced at her feet to see if she was still standing on the ground. She then heard a voice inside her head. It said, 'feel your liberty, angel,' and very quickly Gemma felt her spirit rise. She knew that she was undergoing a profound transformation. When Gemma came back from her meditation she'd changed. It was if she had grown taller and stronger, and she was ready to face anything that came her way!

THE COURT CASE

Tony wished he didn't have to attend Court this morning, because he simply didn't have time, but he'd been asked to be in court with the Barrister. After many discussions with him, he was happy with the evidence and witnesses. Tony wanted a sentence for this man, but the Barrister wasn't sure if it was possible? It was up to the jury to decide whether he deliberately deceived his client by tampering with the contract, or if it was negligence. Even if Alessandro hadn't changed the agreement, it wasn't fit for purpose. Steven, the Barrister, found it hard to believe that a woman like Sylvia would agree to such an arrangement. It certainly wouldn't help her, and there was no doubt in his mind that she'd spent little time investigating his business before investing. Still, it was not for him to question why because this was his work, and he would see the case through to the end. He could only conclude that she must have been drunk, which was something she refused to talk about. Sylvia had also felt insulted by his questions and was very defensive, which wasn't very helpful when he'd been appointed to help her, even if he only got half a story. He would do what he could, but he certainly wasn't a magician. Tony was pleased that he'd pulled in someone competent to help. Steven would carefully examine everything. He also knew that Alessandro would find several character witnesses to vouch for his integrity.

Tony had wanted to pull something new out of the hat. He'd been working for weeks to try and portray a bleak picture of Alessandro. This man was undoubtedly a womaniser who manipulated vulnerable women for money. Tony knew that he needed new evidence, something recent and undisputable.

* * * * * * * *

The Jury assembled in the courtroom, which fell deadly silent as they were seated. Alessandro was walked to the dock to swear an oath, then the Judge informed the jury of the charges, and various statements were read.

The Barrister explained how Alessandro asked his client, Sylvia Jones to invest the sum of ten thousand pounds in his wine business. She'd been advised that for this sum she'd receive a good return on her investment. He continued for quite some time as he made the information as clear as possible to the court. Surprisingly, Sylvia then took the stand herself to clarify what happened. She explained how she'd met Alessandro on a train where they sat next to each other and chatted. She met him later for dinner, and she'd been persuaded that his company was of good standing. Alessandro had also told her there would be a good return on her investment. She explained that she had a genuine interest in wine and had travelled to many of the regions where it was produced. Alessandro promised to return her investment by way of considerable profits that she'd make over the next five years. The jury listened intently to her testimony. Sylvia was extremely clear about her expectations and the terms of the contract and explained how she'd run the idea past her accountant.

Tony had found two witnesses to testify in Court. One of them was a local wine merchant who had paid a deposit of two hundred and fifty pounds for Alessandro to supply wine for a New Year's party. He said that Alessandro let him down and didn't refund his money. The second witness was a woman who sent a cheque to him for five hundred and fifty pounds for astrology charts for her whole family. Alessandro hadn't supplied the charts, claiming they were lost in the post. He'd told her that he would print off copies but he never did. Surprisingly, Tony found both people through his father who had willingly told him that he was always letting people down, and he had no idea what his son did with his time! At least it was something to prove the man was unreliable, but Tony was unsure if it would be enough to convict him.

The courtroom suddenly became hot, and Alessandro looked uncomfortable as he hastily wiped the sweat off his brow. His Barrister started his defence. He told the Court that the business was registered in Italy, not the United Kingdom, which had been explained to Miss Jones at the time of their meeting. Alessandro had worked in the wine business for twenty-five years and that it was normal for him to look for investors. Tony felt that the story was convincing, and it made Alessandro appear squeaky clean. Steven, Miss Jones' Barrister then asked why his client hadn't received the proper paperwork for her investment. He emphasised that in a year, Sylvia had not received any payments although she had helped Alessandro grow his business. Steven then questioned whether the company was in existence. If the figures were correct, then Alessandro would have been in a financial position to make at least one or two payments to his client. He questioned the legitimacy of the contract and explained that although Sylvia had signed the agreement, she claimed that it wasn't the contract she'd signed when she met Alessandro in London.

It was twelve o'clock, and all of Alessandro's witnesses had been called. They all sang his praises and said that he was a man of honour and integrity! One of the witnesses also said he was an excellent businessman and extremely professional in his dealings. He'd made a small investment in Alessandro's business a couple of years ago, after being a customer and friend for many years. The Barrister questioned the witnesses. He wasn't convinced that they had invested in Alessandro's business at all, and he demanded further evidence. The Judge could see where this was heading and asked about the previous year's accounts. He also asked to examine a copy of the contract. He then called for an hour's recess.

Tony felt uncomfortable. It was clear to him that things were not going as they envisaged. He was also annoyed at how good Alessandro's Barrister was. They'd obviously got their act together. Tony knew that if something didn't change, they might well lose the case. Sylvia looked extremely unhappy and was glaring at him across the courtroom.

Steven cleared his throat, 'Your Honour, I know that we've heard some good testimonies from the witnesses, but I would like to draw your attention to the charge of sexual assault made against Alessandro in 2002.'

'Objection Your Honour, the case was several years ago and it was dismissed. It's irrelevant and shouldn't be allowed' Alessandro's Barrister emphasised angrily. A look of horror spread across Alessandro's face as he stared in complete disbelief. Any mention of 'sexual assault' cast a big shadow over him. He had to regain the trust of the Jury.

'Your Honour, will you please let me pursue this line of enquiry. I'm trying to demonstrate the defendant's lack of respect towards women.' continued Steven, who was reluctant to let this go. Then to Tony's complete surprise, some new evidence was given to the Judge to read. Tony stood there waiting to see if Steven could carry on with his line of enquiry, but the judge waved his hand to indicate that he was reading something important. After several minutes the Judge said, 'Ah, we have a new witness to call on behalf of Miss Jones.'

There was a deathly hush in the courtroom. Alessandro's face went deathly white. Once again, his barrister objected and said that it was too late to call another witness but the Judge thought otherwise.

Tony was staggered. What was going on? He'd searched high and low for more witnesses and his enquiries had been extensive. How could he have missed this? They weren't allowed to continue with their line of enquiry because this had taken priority. The weird thing was it felt like this case had a very unpredictable feel about it. Tony felt like he had to just hold on tight because they were being taken on a wild ride! He then heard heels walking along the corridor towards them, and he slowly turned his head. To his utter astonishment he suddenly noticed Gemma his ex-wife! What in God's name was she doing here!

'I call to the stand Ms Gemma Hollesley,' the Judge declared.

Gemma's legs were shaking as she took the witness stand to swear her oath. She didn't dare look at Alessandro, or Tony, but at least the Court got her name right, she thought with a slight grin. Was she in a dream, no-one here appeared real. She found it hard to believe that she was in a Court Room with two men, whom she knew, yet both had suddenly become insignificant. The only thing that felt important to her at this moment was the truth.

Alessandro could not believe it. If Gemma told the court what took place at his house that night after dinner, he would be done for! But why else would she be here? Then he put two and two together. Tony Hollesley the solicitor acting for the bitch, was Gemma's former husband. She'd spoken about him a few times, but he never imagined for one second that he was the Tony Hollesley involved in his court case. Weren't they divorced? He was no longer her husband. She also had her own legal representative.

Alessandro stared at Gemma. There was something different about her. She had the same name, but she didn't look the same. For one, she looked more upright and had grown taller! He tried to clear his throat by taking a swig of water. He was sweating profusely now, and he was scared.

The day had become warmer, and the sunlight was streaming through a glass skylight high up in the centre of the Court Room. Alessandro realised he'd been a fool. His desire for women had turned from passion to abuse. He was now at the end of this road. Playing with a Barrister was playing with fire. Hadn't he done that enough in his life. It was time to stop.

Tony also looked at Gemma. He couldn't believe his eyes. Here was the woman that he was married to for all those years, and he wondered if he'd ever known her. Tony wasn't sure whether he was appalled or thrilled that Gemma had been involved with Alessandro, but he was nonetheless shocked. Now wasn't the time for him to fall apart, he had to compose himself. He was thankful that Gemma had her own representative, and he didn't have to speak to her. Why was she here? He'd just have to wait and see. One thing for sure was this case wasn't going as he predicted.

He looked over at Gemma and was shocked as she began to give the details of when, and where she first met Alessandro. He noticed her whole demeanour had changed. Was she the same woman? She looked more upright, and there was a mysterious glow around her. Light shone on her face, and she no longer appeared real. It was if they were all in a movie. He wanted to run over to her and say, don't do this Gemma. He couldn't understand why he suddenly felt so protective towards her. He also knew that he had to let it go. She was her own woman now, and for the first time, he saw that. Whatever words came out of her mouth, they no doubt needed to. He never used the phrase 'meant to be,' but he was thinking these words now as he stood back and allowed things to unfold magically.

Gemma was pleased that she had appointed her own legal representative. It was necessary as Tony's ex-wife. The Judge had read and considered her evidence, and after a short break, he decided that he'd now hear her statement. It would prove helpful in understanding Alessandro's character. Gemma was surprisingly calm and felt the warmth of her guardian angel with her. She realised that without the support of her counsellor, she would never have made it here. For so long it felt like a nightmare, but in time she became stronger and now nothing was going to hold her back.

Gemma explained to the court the circumstance surrounding her meeting Alessandro. Why she decided to attend the Mind Body Soul event, which led to him asking her to his house for dinner. There was an uncomfortable silence in court, but she continued with her statement along with the help of her solicitor, Hugh Goodfellow, who came from an old firm of solicitors which Gemma had known of for many years. They were her mother's former solicitors and they had an excellent reputation for getting results! Hugh Goodfellow certainly knew what he was doing. He realised that as there were no other witnesses to speak for Miss Jones, it was down to him to cast doubt upon Alessandro's reputation with women, which might be enough to convict him. Hugh understood the court case was not about sexual assault, but he'd persuaded the Judge that Gemma's statement would highlight Alessandro's attitude towards women.

Alessandro's barrister objected once more and disputed the necessity for Gemma's statement. The judge however, told him that he thought it was relevant and overruled him!

Three hours past, and Gemma was tired, but not as weary as she expected because she was carried along by a wave which had gathered momentum. After hearing all the evidence, the judge decided the court would adjourn until 1.30 pm, during which time the Jury would have time to consider its verdict.

At 2 p.m., Alessandro was fined and ordered to pay considerable damages to Miss Jones. They decided to hold him in custody because he was facing a further charge for the sexual assault on Gemma Hollesley! Gemma knew this meant she'd have to attend yet another court hearing, but it was an enormous relief that Alessandro was for now at least, out of the way.

Thank God, he was at last made answerable for his actions. Gemma had grown strong and was proud of herself for seeing this through. As she rose from her seat to leave, Alessandro was being led out of the court. Her solicitor asked her if she was all right. She smiled, then said, 'I think now justice has been done, it's time for lunch.'

'It's time for the rest of your life,' Hugh replied, returning her smile.

Gemma walked out into the afternoon air and noticed the scales of justice on the wall of the Court. The cards were right, she whispered. There has been justice. She was going to make sure that this man was answerable for not only what he did to Sylvia Jones, but for what he did to her, and all the other women he may have damaged. Alessandro needed to see the world through different eyes; women were not there to be controlled or manipulated. Women are intelligent, articulate beings who want to be treated as equals. His Arcadian attitude had no doubt brought him pain and sorrow but he'd learn. She knew that it would be a long time before she felt compassion or forgiveness for what this man had done to her, but it would come eventually. She looked down at her feet and noticed she'd been avoiding the cracks in the pavement like a child! She wanted to laugh. Old habits die hard, she thought. There was still a little time before the girls had to be picked up, so she decided to walk to a small cafe in the town centre.

Gemma sat down and ordered a jacket potato and coffee. The café faced a well-known bookstore. If she had enough time, she'd have a browse at the Tarot and Astrology books. Not that she wanted to buy any more, but she was addicted to looking.

Gemma finished her lunch which was perfect, and enthusiastically walked up the steps to the top floor of the book shop. Getting this episode off her shoulders made her feel lighter. Her counselling had worked well and she was more positive and nurturing towards herself. She was now placed further up her priority list. The days of her nearly setting light to her jeans in front of the fire were well over! She had also made one or two new friends. Gemma had always been good friends with Jo, but there were also a couple of women whom she worked with at the cafe who had recently asked her to go out with them. She felt as if she was starting a completely new life doing the things she wanted to. Her life wasn't perfect, sometimes she still had to watch her pennies, but there were changes. In addition to her cafe job, she managed to pick up one or two readings at home, which brought in some extra money. Things were good. She felt relieved. It no longer felt like some horrible slimy secret, that feeling was vile. If only she'd been able to come forward sooner. However, she'd also been concerned about Tony's reaction towards her. Things had been bad enough between them. Tony was annoyed that he'd asked Gemma to come back and live with him, and she'd once again, rejected him! She knew he was embarrassed about the whole situation. After the court case was over, Tony saw her standing there, and he quickly walked in the other direction. Gemma knew it was his male pride that didn't want to acknowledge her. She walked away with her head held high. She knew she'd done the right thing and whatever he thought, it had a minor impact on her. Tony always sulked when he didn't like something, so it was no surprise to her. For the first time in her life, it occurred to her that she didn't need to be liked. For so many years it felt necessary, but now being in integrity was more important. Yes, she'd grown, and she was starting to like the person she was. She didn't feel so alone. Whatever happened in the court was mystifying but she felt taller, stronger, and somehow lifted. What could easily have been a nightmare had rapidly changed after she told her truth.

She picked up a book by Linda Goodman. It was an old favourite of hers, Sun Signs. She started to read a little more about her chart. After trying to absorb a few pages, she looked at the time on her mobile phone. It was time to make a move. As she stood up to walk away, she noticed a man walking towards her and was astounded to see it was John!

'Hi Gemma, where have you been hiding? I haven't heard anything from you for months. I've painted my lounge; got a new sofa and unbelievably another promotion at work. What have you been up too?' John didn't wait for her reply. Nothing's changed there then, she thought, as John continued. 'The kids are doing great and guess what, I've gone into partnership with Rob, remember him? We're setting up our own design company for logos and websites. He's going to offer the technical stuff, and I'm doing the rest,' he said, unable to get his words out fast enough.

Gemma thought, there he goes again! It's all about him and he isn't interested in my life at all. Good acting though! If only she had realised this sooner, she would have saved herself a lot of heartaches. At least she realised it now, and she was free. A strong feeling of liberty grew inside her, along with a warm glow of pure love. She waited for him to stop talking. She considered mentioning the court case to him, but it was as if the words were stuck in her throat. She realised that it wasn't something that she really wanted to share with him. They had been so close at one time, but now they felt worlds apart.

'You look so good Gem, and what's different with your hair? You look like you've lost weight too. Did you see that astrologer guy in the paper? He ripped off a Barrister or something. You're into astrology, aren't you? Do you know him?' John asked, then waited for her reply.

Gemma nodded her head as if to say she didn't know what he was talking about. It was her business, and the least she said to him, the better.

'Well, come around Saturday night. I'll cook that lovely dish you like. What was it called? Yes, I'll knock that together for us.' John muttered as he glanced at his watch.

'I can't John. Sorry, I'm busy,' blurted Gemma, feeling no regret whatsoever.

'Busy, really? Have you got a date Gem? Tell me who he is?' asked John, sounding a little surprised.

'I have a date with two people actually.'

'Two people?' asked John.

'Yep, I have a date with the two most important people in my life, my children. I'm taking them to see the new Snow-White film,' she said boldly.

'Snow White, all that poison apple stuff,' he replied.

'Yes, I think it is essential to teach them about rotten apples, so when they grow up, they can appreciate how beautiful they are.'

John went silent. He knew he couldn't compete with Gemma's daughters.

Gemma walked away smiling. John didn't see her smile, but Gemma felt a huge grin spread across her face and she broke out in a laugh. If John wanted the relationship with his children that she had with her daughters, he'd have to learn to put them first.' She thought and hurried away.

Gemma was running short of time and rushed towards the car park. She had to get a move on if she wanted to be in time for the girls. She quickly plunged her hand into her handbag and took out her car keys. As she pulled them out, she saw a large white feather fly out of her bag. It drifted slowly to the ground and lay there shimmering on the pavement. The feather was so beautiful she wanted to pick it up, but then decided it was better left where it landed. As she turned the corner, she knew that her future was bright, and some passer-by would soon pick up the feather and discover their own Liberty Angel.

END OF A CHAPTER SYLVIA

Sylvia left the court and immediately called a taxi. How much of her life had she wasted over this crazy situation? She needed to go straight home and bury her head for a while to catch up with work but she felt too tired. With a bit of luck, her colleagues heads would soon stop turning and she'd be able to return to a normal life, if there was such a thing! Right now, she had to phone her daughter among other things, and she needed to get her head in a good place!

Her home office was stacked with work. Sylvia's back ached and she quickly kicked off her shoes and leaned as far back as her large office leather padded chair would allow. The top drawer of her desk was stiff to open and she always kept it locked. God forbid if anyone discovered what was in it! She then carefully spread some white powder in a thin strip along a piece of paper. She certainly couldn't afford to let any of it fall on the carpet. This was their best batch. After several deep inhales it was gone. Thank God, she muttered as her head began to clear of all the crap. Now where's that number? She was aware that they were waiting for her call, and she needed to get this done with, even if she didn't want to communicate, it was necessary.

"How did you get on?" enquired the voice. He's grumpy as usual, she thought. There was never any pleasing them. She needed to get these criminals out of her life!

"Alessandro is going away! It's likely that he'll be gone for a couple of years. As if out of nowhere, a mysterious woman appeared in Court. No one was ready. It was ironic. Can you believe it, she was Tony's ex-wife! To say that he looked shocked is an understatement. This angel looked as if butter wouldn't melt and she had a strange mysterious glow around her. I don't believe in these things, but even I must admit it was very odd. She gave evidence at the last minute and the abuse will put him away. What an extraordinary series of events!

'This woman knew Alessandro?' the voice asked. He found it difficult to understand.

'Yes, he'd managed to pull her into his web of deceit at some health event where he was posing as an Astrologer. Are we even now? You paid my school fees and I got rid of Alessandro. I'll also get my investment back, plus considerable damages.'

'We're pleased with you Sylvia. You did well and despite all the stress, you've come out of it quite nicely. We couldn't have him fouling everything up. He wasn't towing the line. His life was a mess and he didn't care who he dropped in it. We'll be in touch, but for now, just live your life. You're off the hook.'

Sylvia replaced the receiver. What an ordeal. She'd had to plan everything meticulously. The meetup on the train, changing the contract, using all her legal skills to set Alessandro up. The firm thought he was a liability. He was lucky because they usually just disappeared. Alessandro the Astrologer, not even the stars could save him this time! It was odd, there always seemed to be justice, somehow and in some way and it was often unpredictable. Some people would call it an act of God, or divine intervention, but however these miracles came about, it was always demanding work for Barristers. They had to spend hours and hours reviewing everything before they even started putting together something for their clients. Should she pick up the phone to call Tony, but then again, she felt a little out of it. It was unusual to be let off the hook from the firm so quickly. Setting Alessandro up for a few month's school fees felt like a fair exchange, but they wouldn't want to lose her completely, especially as she had friends in high places.

'A mysterious glow,' she muttered, then laughed at herself for repeating it. As if they'd understand, dealing with the firm was like making a contract with the devil! Now, where are my shoes? I need to empty my rubbish before my daughter arrives home.

The key turned in the lock and Beth strode into the house in a cheerful mood. It was half term and to her relief her daughter had a week off school.

'Have you paid the taxi?' asked Sylvia.

'Yes, you gave me the money, remember. It was fifteen pounds but that is the usual from the station.'

'Oh yes, sorry, of course I did. It's been a difficult day. I was thinking, as you hate that school so much, how about we go away for a few months together, France or something? If we like it, we can look for a school over there. We'd have to sell the house of course. Maybe make a fresh start? Your school fees are crazy and if you don't like going there then I don't know why I am struggling every month to pay the fees.'

'I hate it.' Beth replied.

'I know you do darling. I'm so sorry. We'll work something out but let's take a break first. I've friends in France. We can stay with them for a while. We both need change and I need a rest. I'll go and put the kettle on. What would you like to drink? Have you eaten anything?'

'Mum, why have you got a white feather stuck on the centre of your back?'

'What feather?'

'Here it is. It was attached to your jumper. It's an angel feather,' declared Beth, who was smiling. 'It's a sign.'

'So, we look for signs now, do we?' joked Sylvia who was in total disbelief. Is that what they teach you at that expensive school I pay for?'

'No, it's about what they don't teach you,' replied Beth as she gave her Mum a hug.

Liberty Angel

About the Author

Jennifer Lynch is the author of The Silver Lining, William's Wishes, never to be Told, We Hear You Angels and eBooks Attracting What You Really Want and Shades of Kefalonia. She lived her early years in York and Cheltenham and later moved to Suffolk with her family when she was twelve years old, where she has lived ever since. Her mother is the author Gillian Kaye who wrote many historical romance novels. She discovered her writing talent at the age of eleven when she wrote a poem called 'The Street Urchin.' She now enjoys writing books from her home in the Suffolk Countryside. She considers her books to be part of her own healing journey as well as reaching out to others. She runs writer's courses and is an Empowerment Coach.